VISIONS
FROM THE
PAST

VISIONS
FROM THE
PAST

SATYA COLPANI

White Falcon
Publishing
www.whitefalconpublishing.com

Visions from the Past
Satya Colpani

www.whitefalconpublishing.com

The contents of this book have been certified and timestamped
on the POA Network blockchain as a permanent proof of
existence. Scan the QR code or visit the URL given on the back
cover to verify the blockchain certification for this book.

The views expressed in this work are solely those of the author
and do not reflect the views of the publisher, and the publisher
hereby disclaims any responsibility for them.

Requests for permission should be addressed to
satya.colpani1gmail.com

ISBN - 978-1-63640-653-4

In memory of my father who gave me the opportunity to realise my dreams.

'History cannot be written, without confusion, in strict chronological order. It has a natural pattern of progress and pause, of change and absorption, of fact and myth. A legend may be more important in the long run than statistics as a source of action. Growth may be from without or within and its realities are not usually found where they are expected. The illogical must be allowed for as well as the evolutionary because history is a long-term story of human beings in an endless struggle to build themselves a home.'

Marjorie Barnard

Contents

Part Four

Part Five

Part Six

Part Seven

Part Eight

Prologue

One early evening in summer, I sat outside on our balcony, watching the moving water in the ocean rolling gently towards the timeless rocks, washed, and smoothed by the constant flow of the waves. Memories flooded my mind. I remembered when we returned from our overseas trip, and I picked up the phone to listen to the messages. There was a surprise waiting for me.

"Please ring Anna at Terry Estate Agent. I have found a house which will interest you."

The agent took us to a charming brown brick home with gabled roofs, built around 1912. Its original owner was Henry Weston, a well-known cartoonist, painter, illustrator, and architect.

"This might not be the house that appeals to you, but it has a vista of the beach and land surrounded by the bush. The original owner of the house named it 'The Beacon.' Ships used it as a guide upon entering the harbour."

The idea of writing this book first occurred to me when I listened to the many tales and rumours about the people who inhabited Mosman. Amongst them were artists, politicians, intellectuals, and eccentrics. It was not until 25 years later that I decided to explore these ideas, which led me to create Visions from the Past. The people in my book are an essential part of the history of both Mosman and the country. They contributed to the art world, and the development of Australia's early history.

Visions from the Past is loosely based on the life of Henry John Weston (also known as Harry).

Part One

1

Hamburg 1872

Historic photos of Hamburg, Germany in the late 19th Century,

Freddy worked on his father's farm; he was also an artist who painted with watercolours. Once a month, Freddy wrapped up his paintings separately one by one, placed them carefully in his hessian bag, and travelled to Hamburg to see his art dealer.

"Good morning, Herr Weston. What have you got for me? I have a client, who is a wealthy farmer and is looking for artworks for his new farmhouse."

"I have just the paintings for him: two country sceneries, and one of spring flowers." Freddy took them out and placed them on the table one by one.

"Oh! Yes, they are very picturesque and quite large. I think he will like them."

Occasionally, Freddy obtained commissions from wealthy farmers, who liked to adorn their walls with pictures of flowers, sceneries, or portraits of their family. In Hamburg, Herr Weston attended painting classes. When there were no classes, he went to the library, then spent his evening with his uncle and returned home the following afternoon.

On this auspicious day, Freddy stopped to speak to the librarian, Frau Mueller. He had met her several times before and had established a friendly relationship. Freddy needed information on a book he wished to borrow. He suddenly caught sight of a booklet on the table, published by Frederick Busch, the Tasmanian Government's agent for German immigration in Hamburg in 1870.

The title read: The British-Australian Colony of Tasmania. A Handbook for Emigrants, Based on Statistical and Other Official Data of the Royal British Colonial Government (Boyes & Geissler, Hamburg 1870).

Freddy picked up the booklet, and stood there, mesmerised, as if he was holding a shiny nugget in his hands.

He opened the first page, and noticed an advertisement written in German. He started reading it.

"Herr Weston, you can borrow the book. Herr Weston!" the librarian repeated loudly. So intently was Freddy immersed in the poster, he didn't hear her voice.

"Oh!" Freddy raised his head and looked at the librarian. "I am so sorry. Thank you, Frau Mueller." He found a chair nearby and continued reading.

Under Her Majesty's Commissioners.

Entirely Free

EMIGRATION

to

VAN DIEMEN'S LAND

and

NEW SOUTH WALES.

MR. LATIMER, OF TRURO, is desirous of obtaining, immediately, many Emigrants belonging to the class of Mechanics, Handicraftsmen, Agricultural Laborers, Carpenters, Quarrymen, Masons, and Domestic Servants.

The Emigrants must consist principally of married couples. Single women, with their relatives, are eligible, and in certain cases, single men.

The age of persons accepted as adults is to be not less than 14, nor, generally speaking, more than 35; but the latter rule will be relaxed in favour of the parents of children of a working age.

The Colony of Van Diemen's Land has been established more than half-a-century and possesses the usual advantages belonging to the Australian Settlements. It is not subject to drought and affords a peculiar demand for the classes above-named.

NO CHARGE for CHILDREN!!!

Applications post-paid or personal, to be paid to Mr Latimer, 5 Parade, Truro.

Freddy had not seen a booklet about Australia before. He was keen to find out more. When he'd finished reading, he imagined Australia to be a verdant land with green pastures, where he had a plot to grow vegetables, vistas to paint, and adventures to experience.

He thought of his cousin Hans, and his wife, who established themselves in Hobart with a prosperous cabinetmaking business.

Freddy sensed that somebody was standing near him.

"Can I borrow the booklet when you have finished?"

"Of course." Freddy handed the stranger the booklet. "It is very informative."

"Are you thinking of going to Australia?"

"Yes, I am. The Tasmanian government is offering free land to attract German settlers. They need market gardeners and small farmers. And I fall into that category."

"I have been reflecting on spending some time there. I am a scientist and interested in Australian plants and wildlife. The country has plenty to offer, and a wonderful climate. I believe the Sun God lives in Australia."

They both laughed, shook hands, and introduced themselves.

"Perhaps we will meet in Australia," said Ludwig with a smile.

"Perhaps we will."

Freddy, for a long time, considered migrating to Australia and starting a new life. He had learned about this country, rich in minerals, with plenty of wildlife and no shortage of land for growing crops. The migrants from Germany, and elsewhere, had contributed to the country's growth. Freddy's cousin, Hans Peter, had migrated to Hobart and established himself as a cabinetmaker. He now had a shop in Hobart to sell his furniture. In one of his letters, he wrote:

Hobart is delightful. There is plenty of employment. The home construction industry is vibrant. Most English migrants want furnishings and furniture imitating English styles.

Many German immigrants settled in Tasmania, and other parts of Australia. They are in all fields of the industry, from skilled to labouring. Many are professional musicians, painters, and architects. Van Diemen's Island needs more market growers. Sun shines throughout the year. The pristine sea nearby, and white sandy beaches are a sight to behold. We miss the family, and Renate sometimes becomes homesick. She often talks of Martha and hopes that she will come one day.

Freddy hurriedly walked to his uncle's home, eager to discuss his discovery. Freddy was close to his Uncle Wilfred; he enjoyed discussions with him and valued his judgement.

"Australia," said Wilfred, "is a young country offering many opportunities."

"Germany, as you know, is facing many issues. First, we had religious problems between 1850 and the nineties. King Frederick William III's ideology of uniting both the Calvinist and the Lutheran Church to form a new state religion was not popular. The older Germans from Silesia, Brandenburg, and Posen disagreed with his theological ideology. They were persecuted, imprisoned, and their properties confiscated. Many Germans, led by their pastors, packed up their suitcases and left for Australia.

"After King Frederick III's death, we had crop failures, rising prices, and compulsory military service, which made more people want to leave the land.

"I think the changes in the European market generated many disputes. The infiltration of cheap products into the land has affected individual growers in the countryside, as well as individual production. You are still young and should take advantage of what is being offered to you."

Wilfred added, "After 1855, many migrants left for Tasmania from Hamburg. The first German immigrants went to Van Diemen's Land and became prominent pastoralists. Others went to the goldfields in Victoria to seek their fortune. They made a long and harrowing journey crossing the ocean to reach Australia's shores;

some did not make it. All were looking for luck, freedom, and opportunity."

The following morning, Freddy sat on the train, took out his book on Australian history, which he had borrowed from the library, and began reading.

It appeared that England had been thinking about establishing a penal settlement in the Pacific for a long time. The most pressing reason was that Britain needed to offload its criminals, no matter the severity of their crimes. The jails in England were getting overcrowded. At the same time, France was making suspicious journeys to the Pacific, endeavouring to sail around Australia. France appeared to be a threat moving into the Pacific. But Britain got Australia before the French. Freddy wondered what Australia would have been like under the French!

On January 21, 1788, Captain Arthur Phillip, the son of a Frankfurt schoolteacher of German English parentage, had sailed as a Commander of the first fleet to Australia. He guided British ships with convicts to the New South Wales colony, and later, became governor. From 1788 to 1819, Australia was a penal colony used by the British. They settled and isolated their prisoners on a distant shore, away from the general population.

By the time Freddy reached his home, he had decided to immigrate to Van Diemen's Land. Uprooted from Hamburg, Freddy's parents moved to the countryside to create a new life on a farm. They grew potatoes, fruit, and other vegetables. However, the Industrial Revolution threatened the small producers and market gardeners in the rural areas. They combined plots of land to carry out commercial operations, abolishing the traditional farming method. Failed crops and prices for essential items increased by over 50 per cent. Mass manufacturing had taken over individual handcrafted articles.

Freddy considered himself fortunate to sell his paintings, which brought income to support the family. Industrialisation also created wealth for some, who built elegant homes, decorated the walls with pictures, and the interiors with fine furniture. The idea of acquiring free territory in the countryside of Van Diemen's Land and assisted passages was appealing. Australia needed workers to develop the country. The discovery of gold in different states called people from England, Europe, and other parts of the world to work in the goldfields.

With all these thoughts in his mind, as soon as Freddy reached home, he called out, "Martha, Schatz. I have an idea, which I need you to consider with me."

" What is it this time, Freddy? You are always full of ideas."

Freddy smiled. "Come and sit down next to me." He took her hand and kissed it.

"It is something I have been thinking about for a good while. How would you feel about moving to Australia?"

He watched her; she was somewhat shocked, her eyes wide open, her mouth dropped.

"How can we leave the family behind, Freddy?"

"Before you say anything, Schatz, listen to me. You know how difficult it is to establish a living now; prices of food and other commodities are mushrooming. Australia is desperate for farmers, especially market growers. We'll have our own farm in Van Diemen's Land, and our passage is free. Many Germans left for Australia to create a fresh life. We will have land to grow crops and set ourselves up as market gardeners, and of course have wonderful warm and desirable weather instead of the dreary old winter months."

Martha was listening to Freddy, but not without trepidation.

"I have always wanted an adventure, and this would be perfect; to be part of a new country, new challenges, and a better quality of life. Often in the papers, I read of the Germans who settled in different parts of that country, and their success in their newfound land."

"I will never see my parents again." Martha became teary.

"We can take them with us."

"They'll never leave their Heimat, where they have lived all their life. What about your father? He's a pastor and dedicated to his community."

"When we have become successful, we can visit them."

"It will devastate my mother."

"I realise that, Martha, but we need to consider our future and the future of our children. They have two other daughters who would care for them."

She thought about their prospects and the reality of the changes affecting them.

"Well, Freddy if that's what you wish to do, I'll support you and follow you wherever you choose to go. I love you, and you're my husband." Freddy embraced his wife and realised that he could not be without her, and he, too, loved her.

Mr Latimer of Truro advertising assisted migration to Tasmania in the 1850s. Image: Public Domain

2

Van Diemen's Land

Farewell, Farewell,
we wish our land of birth farewell
A land where first we saw day's light
From Hearts all-moved the
parting word is heard
To beloved friends who remain
Farewell, farewell,
we have Van Diemen's Land in View
Yet shall not forget our dear ones
Our prayer for you is sent on high
To see you once again is our desire
Ulric Appeldorff

Joy, hope, fear, and sadness filled Freddy and Martha on the morning of their departure to Australia. They had never been outside of Hamburg and its environs.

Freddy and Martha waited at the busy Hamburg harbour to board the ship, Victory. Around them was a sea of people, chatting, meeting new people, laughing, and crying while waiting to board the same boat for an unfamiliar destiny, searching for hope and freedom. Martha had only experienced life in her hometown of Almhof, where she was born, raised, and married.

He watched the sadness in his wife's eyes, tears rolling down her cheeks, and a feeling of guilt overcame him. He realised how close she was to her family and the sacrifices she was making for him. He took her into his arms to console her.

Angst and the fear of the unknown overcame many women. Husbands comforted them while the children gathered, eager to go on a voyage of discovery. The passengers watched the ship, soon to disappear into the vast ocean. Leaving behind their friends, families, and the country of their birth suddenly became a reality. Young children, excited about travelling on a ship full of bounce and vigour, could not wait to go onboard.

"Freddy," said Martha, grabbing his arm, "we are boarding the ship. It is finally happening." She once again burst into tears.

The journey was long, arduous, and dangerous. Although the passengers travelled on an auxiliary steamer that could cut the sailing time by half, storms were still a common threat. The navigation to Australia was a complex task, requiring the correct navigational tools and dependent on the captain's sound knowledge of the position of the stars at night.

Conditions on the sailing vessel, the quality of the food, the hygiene, and the poor living surroundings, without electricity and refrigeration, caused many deaths, especially on the lower deck. Freddy and Martha settled on the upper deck, with better sleeping areas, lighter, and better food. Freddy kept a diary, written in German, in which he recorded the daily events in writing as well as through his sketches. He also studied English, which filled his days throughout the long and monotonous journey. Martha took out her knitting, a complicated jumper that she was knitting for Freddy, to ease her mind.

When they arrived in Hobart, they were lucky enough to see two familiar faces who welcomed them with open arms. They stayed with them for two days, and then they had to join the rest of the people to travel to Collinsvale.

The Westons received farming land at Collinsvale in the northern end of Hobart's Mt Wellington Ranges. They climbed the hill carrying their goods and chattels on their backs.

When they reached the top of the hill leading to the valley, Freddy said, "Look at that, Martha. How amazing is this valley!"

The beauty of the scenery, still untouched by the hand of civilisation, overcame them. They dropped their goods and sat on the ground, enchanted by the beauty of the place, the vivid and lush greenery, and the undulating grandeur of the mountains.

Appledorff, G, 1938, Valley Collinsvale, Memories of Collinsvale

"The mountains are spectacular," said Martha. They slowly made their way down, until they reached their plot of land. They found a place to put up their tent and settled into their new environment. Some immigrants had arrived earlier and had already set to work building their new home.

The following day, they discovered that the valley had rich and fertile soil, and an abundant supply of clean water from a creek near the Derwent River's tributary. Both Freddy and Martha set to work with local helpers to put up a rough-and-ready home on their farm. First, they cleared the land and built their hut using trees from their part of the land. Next, they constructed the house with thick planks split from the trees, six feet long. They used thick, grown trees without knots, which shed water and kept the hut waterproof. They lined the rooftops with thick pieces of green bark from gum trees to keep them warm during winter. Using dirt, they constructed the floor, and plastered the inside wall with mud to stop the breeze from seeping through the timber slabs.

As soon as Freddy and Martha had enough shelter in the house, they prepared the land and started growing crops. They did not have time to think about the problems they encountered; both got busy with what they needed to do to establish their farm and make a living.

Freddy planted potatoes, carrots, tomatoes, cucumbers, and lettuce. Later in spring, he grew cherry trees, apple trees and created a strawberry patch on a mounded surface for better drainage. Before long, they had established a working farm. Freddy and Martha took their produce to the markets in Hobart on a horse-drawn cart. They returned home, having sold almost all their goods.

What they hadn't sold, they took to Hans and Renate. They often stayed overnight with them and returned the following afternoon.

The Westons had German and Danish friends living near them, and other acquaintances who came to give each other a helping hand from time to time. The men got together with their pastor and built a modest place of worship to attend church services on Sundays. Behind the pulpit hung an unornamented black timber cross on the wall. Handmade dark timber seats lined both sides of the aisles. Every Sunday, the neighbourhood gathered for coffee and cake outside the church and took turns catering for the morning tea. In this way, they could socialise and catch up with German and Danish news and gossip. The men talked of their farms, their products, and their yields.

As time went on, the Westons' farm became prosperous, aided by the rich soil and accessible water. They turned their rudimentary home into a more spacious living space. Freddy added two rooms; Martha used one to set up a sewing room to make clothes for herself. Soon, word got around of her sewing prowess, and people started approaching her to make clothes for them and their children.

Martha created a garden, surrounding her home with a variety of flowering plants. In spring, she planted camellias, peonies, native orchids, and other flowers she learned about through trial and error. They found contentment and, in time, adapted to the new environment. Two years later, Martha gave birth to a son. They named him Henry John Weston.

3

Henry's World

I grew up on a farm surrounded by thickly forested mountain ranges, rolling hills covered in wild native shrubs, giant tree ferns, and native flowers. Mt Wellington was visible from our farm, and in winter, we could see the snow-capped mountain from our valley. I dreamt about going to the snowfields, wondering what it was like to walk on snow and to experience the feel of it in my hands. As a child growing up in Hamburg, when it snowed at Christmas time, Papa told me how the children would throw snowballs at each other. "We built a snowman together with our friends, and sometimes, it was a very tall one. We rolled down a steep hill, then walked up and rolled down again. Sometimes we had competitions of who could do the most runs. It was a lot of fun."

"One day," said Papa, "I will take you up to Mt Wellington, and you can throw snowballs."

I was so excited about going to the mountain looming over us. When the wind blew, it made a sound that echoed through the valley. I often used to dream about it.

Wildlife was abundant around us. There were wallabies, snakes, devils, bandicoots, and a prolific number of birds;

mountain parrots, black cockatoos, plovers, robins, wrens, and many more. My father taught me a lot about the bush, the names of different birds, and to respect wildlife.

"Always watch for snakes; they don't come near you unless you get in their way or if they have young ones near them. Always take a stick with you and make a noise, which gives them a chance to get away."

Warm and caring people surrounded us. Many came from Hamburg and its surroundings in Germany and had much in common; their Heimat food, culture, eating habits, and, often, yearnings. My parents would speak in German to me, as they wanted me to learn their forefathers' language. Papa always said, "We will teach you German, but the country will teach you English."

My father was an artist and an educated man, who had a love for learning and literature. When I was older, about five, he would read me stories from Grimms' Fairy Tales in German, which he had brought with him; but he simplified it for my age.

Papa also realised that I had an aptitude for drawing. Whenever he had some time, especially on the weekends, he taught me how to draw and paint. By the age of six, I sat outside on our veranda when I did not have a playmate and spent time drawing.

I watched the trees, the mountains, and valleys and made drawings in my sketchbook. But, of course, when my friends came around, I would run out and join them and try to find some adventurous activities. Often, we would climb trees, jump down, and go for a swim. Other times, we would walk through the bush to the creek, which took about half an hour, and find a nice shady spot to sit and chatter.

Mostly, we made fun of Rupert, who had a speech impediment; but we were not aware that he had a problem. Whenever Rupert went to the creek, carrying buckets to draw water from the stream, we teased him by imitating his speech. He chased us as far as he could, but then returned to his activity.

When I was seven, I started school at the compulsory age. However, during weekends, my father taught me basic maths and how to read. We had a small village school, and our teachers came from Hobart to give us lessons. After a while, I became bored. Miss Marple kept on repeating the same things, and I stopped listening. I sketched instead. Miss Marple realised what the problem was. She spoke to my parents about it and found out that I had already learned basic maths and could even read. She put me up to a level ahead of me in a class that some of my friends attended.

Walking home from school, I always made a detour through the bush tracks, smelling the flowers and listening to the gurgling creek, with low scrubs and grass surrounding it. I enjoyed my walk from home, sometimes with a friend, other times alone. Often, I sat on the bank and watched the creek meandering down the valley. I listened to the birds chirping and singing and saw wallabies hopping past me.

After four years of primary school, my father sent me to Hobart to the Church of England School as a boarder to complete my primary schooling. At first, I was very nervous about leaving home. I had never been away; the thought of spending the nights in foreign territory for five days of the week with strangers was daunting.

It took me no time to get used to my new environment, surrounded by Australians, and a few foreigners. I enjoyed my school life. They also had art classes, and that was the pièce de résistance. I did well in primary school and gained a scholarship to secondary school. My parents could use the money to put me through tertiary education. Before leaving Germany, my grandfather had given my father some money, which he used to fund my two years of elementary classes and board.

On the weekends, I always returned home. It took me hours of travelling on a horse and buggy. I could not even draw as the riding was rough. I tried to read, but that was also difficult because words always jumped up and down. I had missed our farm and the countryside, and I always looked forward to coming to Collinsvale. When I reached the top of the hill and saw the valley and the majestic mountain, I felt the joy of being home again.

My father was there on horseback, waiting to pick me up and take me home. As we approached our house, I could smell the bread baking outside on our stone stove. Now I felt I was home. My mother was waiting on the veranda, and when she saw me, tears rolled down her cheeks as she came over and hugged me.

Our stove comprised of a pile of rocks with a cavity inside. On Saturdays, my mother would use fire to light it, and when the stones were scorching hot, she scraped the fire out and placed the bread inside. When my mother finished baking the bread, she would bake rock cakes or a currant cake. We would eat the bread at lunch with butter, which was a treat. After lunch, my father would spend a couple of hours with my home-schooling, and then he would have a rest; and in the afternoon, we had cake and coffee. It became a treat, and a ritual in our home. Sometimes we would invite friends to share our afternoon tea. She would then bake some biscuits as well.

Life on the farm was difficult for my mother, and other women. Not only did they care for the family, but they worked on the farm. They cooked outside on an old wood stove or open fire. They washed all the clothes out in the yard and boiled them in a kerosene tin on an open fire in the backyard.

We ate simple food. Jam and bread, bread and dripping, and potatoes were the staple diet we ate three times daily. We made our jam from the fruits on the farm.

We also had a cow which provided us with plenty of milk. My parents sold it to those who couldn't afford a cow, for very little money. As time passed, we all became more successful, as our farms were producing well.

My father bought another acre of land next to his farm and hired two men to work for him. He taught them about farming, which was more accessible because of modern farming tools. Well-to-do investors from the city were interested in buying farms and amalgamating them. He sold one acre of his farm for a fair price and kept the other. The two farmers he had trained took care of the farm.

He had been thinking about moving to Hobart, as my mother's health was failing. It was not the place to be falling ill, as doctors were not easily accessible. The nearest doctor was at Glenorchy, and to get to Glenorchy was a challenging journey on the long and winding road. He also realised how much Martha was missing me.

They bought a small cottage close to Hobart, and we made it our second home. I could now move back home; my mother could take care of me again. My father travelled to the farm three times a week to check on the farm work. When he was home, he worked on the house to improve it. He added another room, which he could use as his studio. The room he was using became a sewing room for my mother. They were also happy to be close to Renate and Peter, who now had two children, and my mother loved having them around.

When I finished school, I had to decide what line of studies to pursue. I was a talented student who excelled in all subjects and could have pursued any available career. But my passion lay in creative arts, architecture, painting, and design. Any spare time I had, I spent sketching. I loved creating cartoons.

My father wanted me to pursue a career in law or accountancy. I told him I wanted to study painting and design, and the best place for it was in Melbourne.

"Why do you need to go to Melbourne to study?" he asked. "We have an excellent art school in Hobart, right at your doorstep. Tasmania has a strong tradition of landscape painting because of the beauty and the charm of the landscapes and seascapes."

"Yes, that's true, but the best art school is in Melbourne for what I want to do. The National Gallery School has courses that interest me. It has the best reputation and would hold me in good stead for the future."

After much debate and discussion, my father relented. My mother organised for me to live with my aunt and uncle in Melbourne—they had migrated there coming from Hamburg. I was pleased to have such a great start, and I promised my parents that I wouldn't let them down.

4

Heidelberg Camp

Roberts, T. 1886, Heidelberg Camp. The Artists' Camp. Image from the National Gallery of Victoria.

I started at the National Gallery School in the summer of 1888. It was also an exciting period in Melbourne, considered the most artistic and cultural city in Australia. Melbourne was keen to establish itself, creating work and money with free settlers, unlike Sydney, the oldest convict settlement.

Therefore, creative spirits flourished because of the economic growth and expansion, and availability of more leisure time. A sense of identity and sentiment of nationalism pervaded all areas of art. The city's lively artistic culture reflected influences from diverse art forms, from the traditional to the modern, such as plein air painting, symbolism, and aestheticism.

However, the National Gallery Art School adopted the European teaching method, and followed traditional painting and composition rules and techniques, or academic rules, to create a predetermined look. A picture is built in multilayer, using thin paint and dark colours, finishing with thicker and lighter tones.

Waking up one Saturday morning, it was a bright, clear summer's day. A gentle breeze was blowing. For a long time, I had wanted to venture into the countryside and explore the campsite at Heidelberg. I packed my bags with some food, painting gear, and a sleeping bag, as I intended to spend the weekend with the Heidelberg artists. Most of these painters had attended the National Gallery Art School in Melbourne.

I caught the tram to Box Hill and was walking towards the campsite, when I heard undecipherable noises coming from a distance. I allowed the loud voices to guide me, as I was sure they could only come from the Heidelberg camp. Drawing closer, I could see a group of men lounging around, having an exuberant conversation over billy tea.

I heard a loud voice.

"Hello, mate, are you coming to join us?"

"Thank you. My name is Henry, and I am from the National Gallery School. I want to learn more about this new art form, which you are all creating."

"You are most welcome. I am Tom Roberts. Come and meet all the budding artists here—we paint together—Charles Condor, Frederick McCubbin, and Arthur Streeton."

"Oh! I have heard a lot about you all."

"Good things, I hope. You don't mind if we call you Harry, do you? It is much easier on the tongue and less formal."

"Not at all, am used to it."

"Come and sit down, Harry, and have a mug of billy tea and biscuit with us. How can we help you?"

"I am very interested in finding out more about the Impressionist art in the Heidelberg School, and its painting style. I have read about French Impressionism and its beginning in France, and how it spread to other parts of Europe."

"At art school, we follow the traditional style of painting." Just then, the artists started to return to their images.

When the artists left, Tom continued, "In order to appreciate what the artists are experimenting with now, it is important to have some idea of what preceded us. Have you studied some colonial art history in class?"

"Not much," I replied. "Next year, we will be doing more."

"English artists who came and settled in Australia painted in a similar style to what you are doing at art school. They had created colonial art and stayed connected to the painting style inherited from their forefathers' places. The Australian landscape, the light, the air, the sky, and the climate were foreign to them.

"Let me tell you about some of the early famous artists who came to this country and brought with them the English style of painting and introduced it to Australia.

"In the early days of Australia's colonisation, pencil and watercolour were used to record official government documentation. However, before 1870, the soldiers, the British naval officers, and unknown convict artists made the drawings. Under naturalist Joseph Banks, Sydney Parkinson, a botanical illustrator, produced the first artistic creation of Australian scenes on James Cook's voyages. These illustrations provided pictorial records of the people, the land, and vegetation, for official government records in London.

"Thomas Watling, I read, was one of the first professionally trained artists transported to Australia in 1792 for committing forgery. As a landscape artist versed in painting English scenes, he found the country's climate and the landscapes disenchanting. The Australian locations completely perplexed him, and he saw himself exiled to arid, unproductive, and uncivilised land, with the light unlike what he was used to painting in Scotland. He found the country devoid of beauty, infertile and the trees he painted in the foreground of his pictures unappealing, affected by fire, twisted in form.

"John Glover was a successful English watercolourist, taught landscape painting in his homeland, and won many exhibition prizes. Glover left his country, influenced by the English press, who painted Van Diemen's Land as an exotic, faraway paradise.

"With his family and many thousands of migrants, he left for Australia and never regretted his choice. His family received a land grant in the northeast part of Van Diemen's Land.

"He was one of the earliest artists who captured the Australian landscape in its pure form. He found the Australian bush unique; the eucalypti, the foliage was unlike the ones in England, and he could capture the Australian outback's essence. Glover particularly noticed that the trees blocked the distant horizons. He had a vast farm and welcomed the Aborigines. He painted them realistically, unlike the previous artists who painted them as Europeans but darkened with burnt cork. He became the best landscape artist of the time in Australia.

"Another eminent painter of the colonial era was Conrad Martens, who studied under Copley Fielding, famous for his watercolours. He came to Sydney in 1835 after taking part in a scientific expedition with Charles Darwin. After an extensive tour with his family around Australia, they settled in NSW. Martens loved Sydney Harbour and its moods and painted atmospheric landscapes. He mostly painted for his patrons and wealthy landowners, but his passion was painting the Sydney Harbour. He worked in watercolour, and his painting of Sydney's view from Rose Bay at sunset is outstanding.

"Now Harry, I know you are keen to learn about this new art form. However, it is essential to know how it evolved."

In our Heidelberg School, we aim to capture the essence of the Australian bush, landscapes, and people through the new art form of Impressionism. We wanted to get away from the realism of the colonial period. Unlike Monet, Heidelberg artists paint in a realist and the plein air style by painting moody twilight scenes and landscapes during bright sunlight.

"The Heidelberg School follows the general style of Impressionism. For example, they used bold, loose brushstrokes, with a lack of clearly defined form. They wanted to create an accurate optical record of colour and light effects. But the artists found the bright chromatic colour used in Europe too extreme for use in Australia. This was because most Australian artists maintained a strong interest in naturalism and a commitment to creating a distinctly Australian style of realist painting that reflected local character and colour. The Heidelberg artists tend to use a more naturalist colour palette. Moreover, in quite a few of our images, we include traditional academic elements such as figures painted with a clear, firm outline."

I stood there, absorbing everything, as Tom explained what the artists were doing.

"I am amazed at the new art movement you are creating. It is all very exciting."

"In 1885," Tom continued, "after I returned from Europe, I was very keen on exploring Impressionism. I wasted no time establishing the Heidelberg School with Arthur Streeton, Charles Condor, and Frederick McCubbin. It was to be a turning point in Australian art."

"I met Streeton on his painting trips to Mentone in 1886. Streeton was only 19 then. He was standing out on the wet rocks, painting there, and I saw his work was full of light and air. We asked him to join us, which was the beginning of a long and delightful association."

"The Heidelberg School is named after the countryside where we spent our time painting. We live in farmhouses and camps and paint the surrounding landscape. We all are serious artists, concerning ourselves with the direction the new art form is taking. We usually escape to our tents at weekends and paint at various locations, executing the plein air movement. The importance of gesture, implemented immediately, impressions of brushstrokes, and spontaneity in our paintings define the new experimental form. We work from early morning through the heat of the day, till noon.

"As more and more artists became familiar with the plein air movement, they established camps in the rural areas around Heidelberg. With broad brushstrokes, shape, form, and colour, the artists created landscapes that were not realistic, where the Australian light typified the country, and they developed their unique style. They camped, painted, and partied. They swam and bathed in the rivers naked."

"Harry," Tom asked, "when you have finished your studies, what are your plans?"

"To begin with, I would like to remain in Melbourne and work to get some experience before returning to Tasmania and taking up a position in Hobart.

"I would like to move to Sydney and work for the Bulletin magazine, producing cartoons and illustrations. It is something I have always wanted to do."

"That is very impressive, Harry, and it is good to have dreams and work towards them. Come with me—I want to show you what I am painting."

We both walked through a winding track, to an area with a creek. Tom Roberts had set up his easel in a shady spot where he worked on his new Sunny South painting. He depicted a nude scene with three naked youths enjoying outdoor swimming and sunbaking.

"Nudity in artworks was against Victorian morals and considered as unsuitable material 'being an act worthy of prosecution,'" said Tom.

"It is a beautiful painting," I said.

"Take out a small canvas, and I will give you some tips about painting in an Impressionist style."

I hurriedly took out my paints and my small canvas. As Tom explained how to create abstract art, I sketched the scenery step-by-step.

"I know you are very ambitious, and you will go far, but two essential things in life are exercise and reading. Read as much as you can, philosophy and the classics. It will help you broaden your mind. Go to the library in Hobart and read, read, read."

Tom's philosophy on life and his love of literature impressed me. I also watched Frederick McCubbin and Arthur Streeton. Their bush paintings captured the characteristics of French Impressionism with their application of paint. McCubbin used flacks and daubs to create foliage and grass, as depicted in his painting of 'The Pioneer'; he dealt with themes of isolation and pioneering struggles against the elements.

McCubbin's paintings, dealing with work and labour and the life of smelly, sweaty, shearing sheds, were not appealing to the wealthy art patrons.

Arthur Streeton called Australia 'the land of the blue and gold.' He loved the Australian landscape, the vastness, and the depth, reflecting light, heat, and sun as seen in his paintings. Streeton received very little professional training. Most training he received was painting outdoors. They considered him the most accomplished colour artist in Australia. At Mentone, he developed his gold and blue palette, which defined essential outdoor Australia.

Norman Lindsay had also spent some months with his friend Moffitt in Charterisville, near Heidelberg, where the Heidelberg artists had painted previously, from 1897 to 1898. They lived in an old cottage and painted nature, in an untended garden. After introducing him to classical artists, his friend Moffitt inspired Norman to paint in his independent style.

Tom had finished working on the Sunny South's painting, which was part of the First Impressionist Exhibition in Melbourne. As I sat down in a grassy spot to observe his work, Roberts came and sat next to me.

"Are there women artists painting in the campsites?"

"Yes, there are. Jane Sutherland and Clara Southern are the most gifted ones who paint with us.

Unfortunately, few women artists painted with the men in the artist camps. They faced many challenges, which hindered them from pursuing a career as an artist. Social conventions of the era prevented women from an overnight stay in the camps."

"I think that is changing," said Henry. "We have several artists in our area, and they seem to do well. Their paintings are excellent."

"Attitudes towards women are changing," continued Tom. "Women previously married and took care of the children, and fully supported their husbands, while receiving little or no support for their interests. But slowly, they took over managing their artworks, organising the exhibition and art unions.

"There are a few powerful women who defied conventions and paved the way for others to follow their path.

"Elizabeth Parsons promotes plein air art and pioneered women artists. She was on the Victorian Academy of Arts council and paved the way for women's future executive positions.

"Mary Vale and Jane Sutherland fought tirelessly in an endeavour to seek professional recognition of women artists. Other women such as Clara Southern and Jane Price were pioneers to gain recognition.

"Both Clara and Jane's success in being accepted in the Victorian Academy of Arts Council and has prepared other women artists for executive positions."

The first Impressionist artworks appeared in plein air painting done on 9x5 inch lids on the cigar box in Australia. The pictures were done quickly, with a thick application of the paint, capturing the fleeting moment according to the ideals of Impressionism. All works were framed and exhibited at the Buxton's Gallery in Melbourne in 1889. The catalogue with the cover designed by Condor explained the art form created.

The critics did not receive the exhibition well. The review in the Argus called Impressionism "a craze, ephemeral in character, and not worthy of attention."

Despite the criticism of their artworks, they sold most of their paintings.

The Heidelberg group of painters were serious artists, concerning themselves with the direction of this new art form. In their attempt to exercise Impressionism, the artists received much condemnation at first because of a lack of understanding. However, as with all innovation, in time, it became accepted. Heidelberg School followed some characteristics of Impressionism, but in much of their works, the influence of realism and naturalism was discernible. The tone of the colour pigments' style appeared more natural and depicted more form in their compositions than Impressionist painters.

The weekend with Tom Roberts, Frederick McCubbin, Charles Condor, and Arthur Streeton was an incredible experience for me. To paint with these talented artists of the future was remarkable. These were exciting people, but different. While Roberts was the main instigator of the movement, others brought their personalities into their creations.

I found it interesting to analyse these characters. They all had a unique name. Fred McCubbin, known as the 'Prof', was grounded, with his sincerity and feeling for the human story. Arthur Streeton, known as 'Smike', was young, volatile, with a romantic touch and a sparkle. Charles Condor, known as 'Kay', had a feminine element about him, and they knew Tom Roberts as 'Bulldog', a leader.

In the evening, we sat around the campfire. It was Arthur's turn to cook the meal, which was chops and potatoes, and boiling the billy. They would take out their pipes, and discussions on world affairs would inevitably happen. There was music and laughter. Tom Roberts played his tin whistle, McCubbin sang in a mellow voice, and a great camaraderie existed between the men. At the end of the evening, they looked forward to another day of discovery, exploring and painting undiscovered Australian landscapes.

The next day, I joined Tom Roberts again, and finished my painting. In the afternoon, I took my leave with a promise to return. They bade me goodbye and wished me well with my studies. I sat on the tram, reflecting on my weekend—the campsite, the interesting men I met, and their contribution to the future of art in Australia. I returned home with a feeling of having experienced another world.

After finishing my studies, I stayed in Melbourne and joined Blamire Young and Lionel Lindsay. I worked on posters, famous ones being Dunlop Rubber, London Tailoring, and Boomerang Brandy. At the same time, I worked on my postcards and signs, which the Victorian art Society exhibited. I became part of it and member of the Melbourne Prehistoric Order of Cannibals and the Bohemian Sketch Club Society. Most members were young students who gathered monthly, painting and making sketches and generally having a good time.

Watling, T. 1794. View Sydney Cove, image from the Library of NSW

Glover, J.1838. River Nile, Van Diemen's Land, painting from the NGV

Martens, C. 1840. Aboriginal Camp site, National Gallery Victoria

Roberts, T. 1887. The Sunny South, Mentone, (Victoria) National Gallery of Victoria

Roberts, T. 1887. Slumbering Seas, Heidelberg Collection, NGV

Streeton, A. 1896. "The Purple Noon's Transparent Might,"
Mentone NGV

McCubbin F. 1907, Lost National Gallery Victoria

Charles C. 1889, Summer idyll, National Gallery of Victoria

McCubbin, Frederick. 1884. The Letter, Public Domain

5

Goldfield

The night too quickly passes.
And we are growing old,
So let us fill our glasses
And toast the Days of Gold.
When finds of wondrous treasure
Set all the South ablaze,
And you and I were faithful mates.
All through the roaring days!

Then stately ships came sailing
From every harbour's mouth,
And sought the land of promise
That beaconed in the South. Then southward
streamed their streamers
And swelled their canvas full
To speed the wildest dreamers
E'er borne in vessel's hull.

Their shining Eldorado,
Beneath the southern skies,
Were day and night forever
Before their eager eyes.
The brooding bush, awakened,

Was stirred in wild unrest,
And all the year, a human stream
Went pouring to the West.
ROARING DAYS BY HENRY LAWSON 1889

In 1851, the history of Australia changed with the discovery of gold in NSW and Victoria. It was no longer a country of just ex-convicts, sheep breeders, wool, and wheat producers, but a land of opportunities, fortune hunters, and freedom to pursue a new life. From all over the world, immigrants came in hordes, digging the grounds in search for gold. Many had money, were educated, and brought with them radical ideas. With the discovery of gold came financial benefits to the cities. The country prospered, more buildings were erected, businesses boomed, and towns soon became cities.

At the end of my studies and before starting work, I wanted to experience life outside my world. At art school, I had come across the von Guérard Diaries, with sketches from the Victorian mines, and found his Australian oeuvre fascinating.

Eugene von Guérard, already a recognised artist in Germany, sailed on the Windermere, one of the eight ships destined for the Victorian goldfields. Coming from a background of European academics, and the De Guérard's aristocratic family, with the family's wanderlust history, it is not surprising that Guérard made the long journey to Australia. He arrived in Geelong in January, 1852 and soon made his way to Ballarat.

Guérard recorded his life in the goldfields in his sketchbooks, which he religiously carried with him. He continuously made notes and drawings, despite working long hours and rushing from one strike to another; surrounded by dirt, flies, scorpions, and giant black ants in his bed, and covered in sweat in all weather. It was remarkable to find his diary, which provided visual and written records of Victoria's most informative and exciting period.

In 1853, discovering the gold nuggets enabled Victoria to become commercially viable, and not only known for grazing sheep and as a "cabbage" patch for NSW.
The gold discoveries also brought about the growth of artistic and other cultural activities.

Although life and the conditions in the goldfields had disenchanted von Guérard, with people living in squalor and the prevalence of crime, greed, and racism, he continued to write, sketch, and paint prolifically. Not only did he provide a significant record of the most buzzing period in the history of Australia, but he also presented it with a wise vision and humour. Unlike the former artists who only saw the colonial scene through European eyes, von Guerard could identify with the country, with a little understanding of the land. He had experienced life in the goldfields, dug the earth, lived a life that became part of him and touched his soul. He had adopted Australia as his home for 30 years. He travelled throughout the country, painting and sketching caverns and cliffs, destruction of Eucalypti caused by storms and bushfires, and the vast fig trees with branches smothered by wild vines:
"He recognised the peculiar light, the long distances, the low horizons, and the wide expansion of the sky. The lonely, unexplored, virginal places in which he could commune. Nature haunted him. He found pleasures in

the pathless woods and rapture on the lonely shore. If the Romantics have influenced his art, Alexander von Humboldt had been his guiding star."

In 1870, he was appointed Master of Painting at the National Gallery School of Victoria but remained there for only a year because of ill health before returning to Europe. Other artists, such as S.T. Gill, produced albums for engravers, depicting the daily lives of the diggers on the goldfields. He was one of Australia's first commercial artists and draughtsmen, photographer and eventually became the first-grade lithographer and engraver.

I, too, wanted to follow von Guérard's footsteps, fulfilling my yearning for adventure, and spend three months in Kalgoorlie, located 595 kilometres east of Perth. Mines in Western Australia were newly opened, without much infrastructure in the mining areas. I mentioned my desire to go to Western Australia's goldfields to my good friend Joe, who was in my art classes.

"I would love to do something like that," he said excitedly, and in the same breath, "I'll come with you."

"Brilliant."

"Let us get together and organise it," said Joe, beaming. "My father has a friend who works there, and I am sure he will help us. He is a good man."

I wrote to my father to let him know what my plans were. At first, he thought I should not waste any time and start working straight away. There were lots of opportunities in Tasmania waiting for me. But, on the other hand, it would be a valuable experience for me to see a different world, which required hard labour under challenging conditions.

"However," he said, "if that's what you wish to do, go ahead."

The gold rush in Western Australia was one of the most defining periods in Australia's history. It brought wealth, democracy, social change, and multiculturalism, and reshaped the environment.

The discovery of rich alluvial gold deposits near Mount Charlotte in 1893 in Western Australia brought migrants from all parts of the world, searching for their treasure in Kalgoorlie. By 1903, Kalgoorlie's gold rush had begun. With the discovery of a 9-pound gold nugget, the diggers wasted no time in frantically demarcating mining areas for diggings. The population of Kalgoorlie had increased to 30,000, with 93 hotels and eight breweries.

Golden Mile. 1895. Eastern Goldfields, Historical Society

With Australia still an undeveloped country, mining towns had to be established, and the supply of water was limited and unclean, which brought about many deaths from typhoid. The water shortage led to the establishment of water desalination plants, with owners selling water at a much higher price. The miners' food supply was limited, and they were forced to eat overpriced 'tinned dog', Australian slang for tinned meat. Life was tough, and miners were working in harsh conditions, with many dying of diseases.

It was a long trip to Western Australia. We took another train from Perth, which took five hours, and we arrived at the Kalgoorlie station in the early afternoon.

Tommy, a friend of Joe's father, met us at the station. He generously offered us his tent at the campsite and took us into town first to organise a mining permit. The camping site was close to the goldfields. We had brought some food supplies with us, including a large water container.

The next day, we walked into town to purchase digging utensils and stock up food. Tommy gave us instructions regarding the procedures involved in claiming a mining site and gold prospecting techniques, such as panning and cradling. We looked at each other, somewhat bamboozled by the protocols we had to follow. We expected just to arrive there, get a couple of utensils, find a spot, and start digging.

"Sunday is not crowded like it is during the week," said Tommy. "So, this is an excellent time to set up your mining plot. If you need any help, just come up to the office next to the bank."

We thanked him for his support.

"What a nice man he is. We are certainly fortunate. How does your father know him?" I asked.

"He worked in the same engineering company as my dad. He left a few years ago in search of adventure and found it in Kalgoorlie. They both kept in touch with each other."

We spent the rest of the day looking around the area and making sketches. Shops, hotels, pubs, a couple of banks, and a gold trading shop lined the street. Joe remarked, "That's where we will go when we get our big nugget," pointing to the shop where gold was traded. "It will set us up for life."

We made lots of sketches. The goldfield mines started about three kilometres from the camps. We hired a horse and buggy each to take us to our base.

The following morning, we both woke up early, excited and ready for the adventure of a lifetime. After breakfast, we packed our bags with food and a large amount of water. We mounted the horses and arrived at the goldfields, which extended for miles. We rode for about three kilometres before we found a small patch of unoccupied land near the creek, which we claimed, marked, and started digging in. A couple of old diggers passing by noticed we were not very skillful in how we were going about digging for gold. They stopped to show us how to start prospecting:

"Crikey! What are you two boofheads doin'?" said the digger.

"Oh, good morning, we're new to the goldfields, it's our first day, and I'm not sure we know where to start," said Joe a little sheepishly.

"Well, it looks like you two couldn't organise a piss up in a brewery!" roared another of the diggers, his face bright red with what looked like a combination of sunstroke and years of exposure to the elements.

"Let me give you a bit of advice," he continued. "Bring those shiny new tools over here and let me show you how it's done."

Over the next half hour or so, the old diggers kindly gave us a crash course in prospecting. The men were quick to laugh at our expense, but they were also well-meaning, and generous with their knowledge. It was precisely the guidance we needed on our first day in the fields.

"Ok, you wombats, time to give it a go for yourselves. Stop bludgin' and get into it."

The diggers gathered their belongings and started on their way before one of them yelled over his shoulder, "Oi! If you boys strike it rich, then remember, the coldies are on you!"

We replied in unison, "Sure thing," and thanked them profusely before turning to one another and laughing with excitement.

We continued digging every day, consumed like the rest of the miners with gold fever. A week later, we both caught sight of something shiny. We started digging with enthusiasm at the sight of this apparition until we extracted a pea-size nugget. We could not contain our excitement. An old passer-by stopped to see what was causing all the commotion.

"Strewth! What a ripper!" he announced with glee. "Looks like you boys are having some beginners' luck. Let me have a geek."

The digger held the fragment up to the sun, squinting at it like a forensic surgeon.

"Just be sure you keep this under your hat, for now. Most bastards around here are gutless wonders. They'd swipe their granny's treasured jewellery given half a chance!"

The passers-by had plenty of well-meaning advice for us.

"There's all kinds of skullduggery to look out for in these parts," he warned, "and the cops aren't much help either, unless you can slip them a backhander, if you know what I mean. Be sure to take that little goldie to the trading shop at day's end and chuck your dough straight into the bank before any anyone cottons on."

As time passed, we collected a few tiny pieces of gold dust. We started digging with enthusiasm. We continued to explore. At the end of the week, we found some more gold dust. We took our find to the gold trader. With the exchange we received, we made enough money to pay for the food and the utensils we had bought, which would last for the rest of our time in the goldfields. In the evenings, we made sketches of the surroundings and life in the goldfields. I was looking forward to making cartoons of the characters we came across on my return to work.

Sunday was a day off. Joe and I walked around the campsites, sketching the surroundings and the landscapes. Miners were dressed in their Sunday best to go to church. Children were outside, happily skipping and playing games. Women wandered around the shops with their husbands.

On Friday evenings, we would join the other miners and enjoy the camaraderie we experienced in the pub. We heard many tales of the diggings. Some were thrilled with their finds; others, even if they did not have a catch, still lingered on, hoping that they would eventually be successful. There were tales of violence amongst the miners. Fights, shootings and killings, and inebriated behaviour often occurred.

One digger greeted us with a long beard and a stomach like Pinocchio's nose.

"G'day fellas, ain't seen youse round 'eer before. What's your story?"

"We have come from Melbourne," said Robert, "but I am originally from Tasmania."

"Melbourne!" replied the digger. "You won't get into any trouble down there. What do you boys do for a crust?"

"We both have been studying art and design."

"You mean drawin'?"

"Something like that."

"You mean painting nude ladies, ay?" he said with a wink and a nudge. "There's plenty of those behind the bar here. A bit rough around the edges, but they scrub up all right."

"Anyway," he continued, "if it's the big bucks you're after, then you've come to the right place. It's hard yakka, but keep diggin' boys, you'll find some nuggets—plenty around."

"Ok, fellas, I'm knackered, time for me to get some shut-eye.

Early start tomorrow, might even see youse out there."

We returned to our tent, as we also wanted to start early.

After two months in the burning heat of the day, eating food just to keep us going, and collecting a few more gold specks of dust, we returned to Melbourne. The time we spent in the goldfields instilled memories in our minds forever. I sat down and wrote a letter to my parents.

Dear Mamma and Papa,

I am back in Melbourne, having had the most incredible adventure and experience of my lifetime. I met many people from all parts of the world. It was not comfortable spending all day in the fields digging and digging, and most days were fruitless. But when we had a find, even if it was a minute piece of gold, we were elated. I am sure everyone heard our screams and shouts. I took photos and made many sketches. Joe and I had a lot of fun together. We met some generous and humorous Australians, always eager to lend a hand.

I have found an apartment with Joe, in Melbourne, and am preparing to exhibit a series of goldfield sketches. At the same time, I got a job to do some cartoons for the Bulletin.

Blamire Young and Lionel Lindsay have asked me to work on Dunlop Rubber, London Tailoring, and Boomerang Brandy posters. I joined the Melbourne Prehistoric Order of Cannibals and the Bohemian Sketch Club Society. Most members are young students, gathering monthly, painting, making sketches, and generally having a good time.

I will take a couple of weeks off to visit you soon.

Your loving son,

Henry

At the end of 12 months, I received news from an architect's firm in Launceston, where I had applied for apprentice architect work, confirming my acceptance. I wrote to my parents, gave them the news, and told them that I would spend Christmas with them.

Von Guerard, Eugene. 1954. 'I have got it.' Oil on paint.

Gill, S.T. 1864. The New Gold Rush. Victoria, NGV

Gill, S. T. 1818-1880. Digger's Wedding in Melbourne. NGV.

Part Two

6

The Wedding

There was an explosion of excitement at the Callaway household. Ruth Callaway was getting married. It was a society wedding with 200 guests at their property in Launceston. Ruth's father had established himself as a dairy farmer, employing several men on his farm and, through hard work, become successful.

I met Ruth in Launceston before I left for Melbourne again. Daphne, a close friend of Ruth who got to know me through work, invited me. She was very keen on introducing me to her.

"Ruth, I have found a perfect match for you. I think you will like him," said Daphne.
"Tell me more about him."
"Well, he is good looking, tall, slim, and very smart."
"How smart is this tall and handsome man, and how did you meet him?"
"I met Henry when he was working at the Launceston Architects Office as an apprentice. Later, he left to take up a position as a staff artist on the Launceston Examiner,

and we kept in touch. He studied art, architecture, and design at the Melbourne Art School. He also had an exhibition at the Launceston Art Society and sold many of his paintings. He invited me to the opening of the collection."

Ruth became curious to meet this man about whom Daphne spoke so glowingly. Perhaps, she thought, he might have been taking out Daphne. Then she realised that Daphne already had a friend. Just then, Henry made a grand entry, perfectly dressed in a suit and looking quite suave. Daphne went to the door and greeted him. "Come with me. I would like you to meet a special friend of mine."

When I met Ruth, the attraction was instant and mutual. Amidst our conversation, my ex-colleagues started approaching me. I had to catch the train to Hobart early the following morning and regretfully left the party after dinner. However, before leaving, I spoke with Ruth and said that would be in touch.

A week later, I wrote to Ruth from Melbourne

Dear Ruth,

I am sorry I did not have enough time to spend with you and converse with you. Since being in Melbourne, I have had a hectic schedule designing posters for a well-known company. I have enough work here to last until the end of the year. The art scene in Melbourne is fantastic and thriving. I am meeting up with friends and artists, some from my class and others from the Bohemian Club, which I joined during my student days.

We gathered in the club, painting and exchanging ideas. Some of them since then have become well-known artists. I have designed some posters for Dunlop Rubber and Boomerang Brandy.

I will be back in a few months, and I hope to see you then. How are your studies going?

Keep well,

Henry

Ruth was excited when she heard from Henry. She rang Daphne immediately.

"I received a letter from Henry."

"I am glad to hear this! You will reply, won't you?"

"I do like him," remarked Ruth.

A few days later, she wrote:

Dear Henry,

I was pleased to hear about you and your work. I have started teaching class four students at the Sacred Heart College for girls, and I immensely enjoy my work. It is my first year of teaching. I am staying at my aunt's place with my cousins and am very comfortable here.

Melbourne sounds like an exciting city. You must have fun as well as work.

I am looking forward to seeing you again.

Warm wishes,

Ruth

As soon as I returned to Hobart, I telephoned Ruth and asked to meet the following Saturday.

"I am staying with my aunt and two cousins," she replied. "My cousins have invited me to a ball on Saturday evening."

She paused for a few seconds and hesitatingly asked, "Would you like to join our table? We do have space for another person who couldn't come at the last minute."

"I would like that very much."

Ruth went to her cousins, sitting outside on the veranda, relaxing. "Who was on the telephone?" asked Maud.

"Henry," she said with a smile.

"What did he say?"

"He wants to take me out for dinner next Saturday evening."

"But we are going to the ball."

"Yes, I told him. I invited him to come to the ball, since we have a spare place at our table."

On hearing screams of laughter coming from outside, Ruth's aunt, who was preparing dinner, came out to investigate the commotion.

"Oh! Mummy, Henry has invited Ruth for dinner next week, and as Ruth is coming to the ball with us, she has invited him to the ball!"

"Oh!" said Aunt Lucy, "well, that is a surprise."

"Aunt Lucy, I have got nothing to wear," said Ruth.

"We can go shopping tomorrow, and I am sure you will find something suitable."

"I will ring Mummy and let her know, and she will reimburse you when she is in Hobart."

The following day, they arrived at the shop. A well-dressed, buxom lady, in a cream suit, greeted them.

"We are looking for a ball gown for my niece," said Aunt Lucy. "We would like to look around first and see if we can find something Ruth likes."

"Certainly. I will just point you in the direction of the ball gowns for her age group."

"Thank you." They all walked over to the pointed direction and looked at all the beautiful dresses in pinks, creams with frills, laces, and fitted, voluminous skirts.

Ruth looked at all the frills and ruffles and was overwhelmed.

"Such beautiful gowns!" exclaimed Ruth. "I will have difficulty choosing one."

Finally, having tried a few, Ruth found a dress she liked.

"You look like a princess!" remarked Aunt Lucy.

"That dress is exquisite," said Jane. "It suits your dainty shape."

"True," said her aunt. "It looks as if it was tailored just for you."

Freddy and Martha were anxiously waiting for Henry's return to Hobart, and they were happy to see him and have him home at last, even if only for a short time, before he left for Launceston.

Freddy had a plan for Henry, which he wanted to discuss before leaving.

"Henry, would you like to take over my shop and establish your business?"

"What will you do?"

"Your mother has a lucrative business with her sewing, and she is enjoying it. I can continue to paint from home. We want to travel and enjoy our life after years of hard work."

"What a wonderful idea, dad."

"We would like to go to Hamburg and see our family and other relatives. They are waiting for our visit."

"Regarding your studio, dad, I could convert half the office to exhibit paintings, posters, and pictures, and the other half will become my workshop."

"Well, that sounds like an agreeable answer," said Freddy. "Hobart is growing, and you won't have trouble finding work."

On the evening of the ball, the girls were full of excitement, their voices rising to a crescendo. They arrived at the ball with their cousins and friends. Henry was standing outside the entrance, waiting, in his black-tie attire.

"He looks so elegant," Ruth thought and approached him with both excitement and nervousness. He greeted Ruth with a kiss and handed her a red rose in a box.

"Thank you. What a nice gesture."

"You don't have to attach it to your dress. You look beautiful and your dress suits you."

Ruth felt instantly drawn to Henry. His manner was that of a gentleman, she observed. He was attentive and made her feel comfortable without being overbearing. After the introductions and settling in their seats, Henry wanted to know all about her.

"I always wanted to work with children and was fortunate enough to study further and become a teacher," said Ruth, "in contrast to many other girls, who were forced to stay home and eventually marry, even though some would have preferred to attend school. Many women's lives revolved around domestic duties, raising a family, and becoming their husband's property. It is not a life for me."

"How do you feel about women wanting to work or study?" she asked.

"I am all for it. We have had quite a few female students studying art, and they were excellent in their achievement. Women should be allowed to study and do what they desire."

"I want to be useful and do something for the benefit of society. I am also involved in a women's group outside school. I believe in women's equality; they should have the right to vote, and to choose a career path, be it in politics or in whatever field they wish to pursue."

It surprised me to hear Ruth's opinion. Most of the girls I met in Melbourne were keen on finding a husband and getting married.

"What about marriage and children?" I asked.

"Of course, I want to get married and have children, but that doesn't mean that we can't be useful otherwise. My father encouraged us, his three daughters, to pursue higher learning when education was not a priority for women. He is a wonderful and devoted father and is also involved in helping the poor and the needy. His family is his number one priority. I think I have inherited his nature for caring for the underprivileged and those in need."

"We have similar parents," said Henry. "I am the only son they have. My parents wanted more children, but they couldn't. They have been very devoted."

"As far as women's progress, change is gradually taking place," continued Henry. "More girls are going to school now. Women are getting more and more involved in seeking equality."

Ruth was happy to hear that Henry had similar views as she had.

Just then, the music started playing again.

"Would you like to dance?" I asked.

"Yes, I would love to. My parents made me go to dance classes. 'When you attend a ball or a dance, you must be able to dance. You don't want to be sitting down like a wallflower,' my mother used to say."

"I don't think you will ever be sitting like a wallflower for too long," I said, looking at Ruth with a smile.

We danced until the music finished, returned to the table, and sat down.

"Tell me about yourself," said Ruth.

She listened to my story with great interest.

"It must have been difficult for your parents to leave behind their families and homeland and start from the beginning in Australia. I would love to meet them. Tell me more about Melbourne—what did you study there?"

"I chose to study art, design, and architecture in Melbourne. I wanted to go to a particular college.

After I had finished my studies, I travelled to Western Australia with a friend for three months to work in the goldfields."

"Goldfields," said Ruth, "that's adventurous. What was that like?"

"An incredible experience! I was lucky to have Joe with me. We met some Australians, ready and eager to help us. Of course, there were people from all over the world. One day I will tell you more about it.

"I took up a position in a design company for 12 months to gain some experience in Melbourne. At the same time, I worked on a collection of sketches, paintings, and cartoons that I had done at the goldfields. The Victorian Art Society invited me to hold an exhibition of my works with them, which was successful. While I was in Melbourne, I joined the Prehistoric Order of Cannibals and the Bohemian Sketch Club Society; most members were young students."

"These clubs sound unusual. What kinds of things are happening there? It sounds as if you were practising cannibalism."

I laughed. "Bohemianism was a trend of the 19th century, which originated in France and reached other cities in Europe and America. It promoted heavy drinking, a life of poverty, and devotion to painting and appreciating art. However, in Melbourne, it took a different road. The Bohemian Club became a club for well-to-do men who pursued philosophy, hard drinking and not experiencing any hardships and poverty. I was able to meet a few artists of the future, such as Norman and Lionel Lindsay, both artists from Sydney. My next move will be to Sydney shortly."

Ruth listened with great interest to my achievements.

We saw each other almost every evening, and at the end of the week, I invited Ruth to my parents' home for dinner, and they were suitably impressed. I spent the following weekend at the Callaways' home. Mr Callaway invited me to his workroom, an exceptional place to escape from the hustle and bustle around him. It was his inner sanctum, and he rarely asked anyone to join him there.

Twelve months later, I proposed. Ruth was overjoyed. She found the man of her dreams; thoughtful and gregarious, with a great sense of humour. When Ruth came home, she went straight to her mother.

"I have some news to tell you."

"Indeed, what news might that be?"

Observing her face, with eyes sparkling and a little blushed, she knew it would have to be something special.

"Henry has proposed to me."

When Maud and Emily heard the news, they could not contain their excitement. The sisters hugged each other, and Mrs Callaway came over to Ruth, took her in her arms, and kissed her forehead.

"May you be blessed with a fulfilling life with Henry."

"When will the wedding happen?" asked Maud. "Can we be your bridesmaids?"

"Yes, I was going to ask both of you. Will you two be my bridesmaids?"

"Of course, we will!"

"Where is Henry?" asked Mrs Callaway.

"He is in the garden with dad," replied Ruth. "He is asking for his blessing."

Just then, both men came back inside in high spirits.

"Mummy," said Ruth, "I would also like our cousins, Jane and Olivia to be my bridesmaids. Henry has asked his friend, Joe from Melbourne, and his cousin from Hobart to be his groomsmen."

"Is he the one with whom Henry went to Art School?" Emily inquired.

"Yes, that's him."

Joe was teaching at the art school in Melbourne, which he enjoyed, but he was still uncertain about his future. I phoned Joe and asked him to be my groomsman.

"Congratulations, Henry. It will be my pleasure."

"Once we have decided on the date, I will let you know. I would love to take you to our farm in Collinsvale, where we can spend a couple of days before the wedding."

On the day of her wedding, Ruth woke up early. She was both nervous and excited. She took an early morning walk on her family property. Breakfast was ready, and the family were all seated at the large timber table, chattering with relatives who had come from Hobart and Melbourne. They were all staying at the Callaway country mansion.

Mr Callaway went outside and hugged his daughter and wished her much happiness. He wanted to see her one more time before she got wedded.

Ruth was close to her father and had inherited many of his traits. He was warm and caring, a devoted family man, and much involved in his community.

"Where is Ruth?" asked Mrs Callaway.

"She went for a walk," called out Mr Callaway as he entered the dining room.

"I'll go fetch her," said Maud.

"I'll come with you," said Emily, the youngest of the Callaway girls.

After a short walk within the property, the girls found Ruth, enjoying a peaceful moment, examining the spring flowers in bloom. Ruth saw them and ran over to hug them.

"What are you doing here?" asked Maud.

"I am enjoying the fresh air, the environs, the silence, and reflecting on the happy times we have had in these beautiful surroundings. I will miss you both very much."

They all became tearful and hugged again.

"Come on, let's go; everyone is waiting for you at breakfast," said Maud.

"We have a hairdresser's appointment at nine—don't forget, girls—and then a makeup session," said Mrs Callaway. "You better not linger too long at the breakfast table. Both ladies will be here in half an hour."

The wedding took place in St Martin's Church, well-known to the Callaway family. They attended the service there every Sunday morning. All their children were baptised and confirmed in this church.

Ruth looked spectacular in her lengthy, cream, narrow-waisted dress, trimmed with lace and Bebe ribbon. It had a frilled bodice, with a high neckline and puffy sleeves, that tapered into the wrist. She carried a sheath-shaped bouquet filled with white roses, orange blossoms, lilies, and orchids.

The Launceston Examiner, where I was working as staff, wrote:

"A Wedding, which created a considerable interest, took place at Wynyard on Monday, the contracting parties being Mr Henry Weston of Hobart, and Miss Ruth Callaway of Table Cape. Mr Weston is well-known in Northern Tasmania, having been engaged as an artist on the Examiner staff. It has been some years since he moved to Melbourne, where he has established an extensive connection. The happy couple received many congratulations, and a trip to England, it is understood, is contemplated shortly.

They held a reception and tea party after the ceremony, with many guests being present; after this, the bride and bridegroom left for Burnie, en route to Launceston, amid showers of white flowers and old boots. Numerous and hearty were the expressions of good wishes for their health and happiness.

The bride is a great favourite at Wynyard, ever ready to lend help in matters of social interest, remarks our correspondent. Her departure will be greatly missed."

After the wedding ceremony, the Callaways held a gala reception at their property, and a week later, the Westons left for London for their honeymoon.

7

Europe

Henry and Ruth sailed from Hobart on a large steamship, minimising days onboard the ship to 50 days. Vessels were less reliant on winds, which allowed them to travel at a constant speed while generating power for electric light, refrigeration, and ventilation. They had a small cabin, with a view of the outside, and a large deck where passengers could spend their time playing games and sunbathing. In the evenings, after dinner, people from the boat's upper echelons would gather in the dance room for an evening of dancing and entertainment.

Ruth was excited about meeting some of her relatives. They were also looking forward to seeing the newlyweds. They spent a week in the city, and then travelled to the town's outskirts to meet some close relatives. Henry spent a great deal of time visiting the galleries. His first trip was to the National Gallery with Ruth. Other times, he went on his own, leaving Ruth to wander around the city with her cousin Anne, a nurse, who was eager to learn about Australia and had dreams of moving to Sydney and working there indefinitely.

Henry was more interested in looking at art galleries in London. He had seen the prominent artists' works in art books and studied some of them intensely in history class but standing in front of the paintings and seeing them was exciting. There were paintings from Turner, Hogarth, Thomas Gainsborough, Degas, Titian, and Velazquez, all masters and forerunners of Impressionism.

Then there was a section on the Renaissance artists, and early Renaissance works from 1400 to 1490, by Fra Angelico and Sandro Botticelli, who started experimenting with realism. Filippo Brunelleschi discovered linear perspective, the idea of all parallel lines converging to one point.

Between 1490 and 1527 came the High Renaissance period, with Leonardo Da Vinci, Michelangelo, and Raphael. It was the scientific works of Da Vinci which allowed him to invent aerial perspectives. In one of his paintings, Henry observed that making the blue's wavelength shorter than the other colour in the spectrum creates an illusion of distance.

He studied Mona Lisa's painting and could see the technique of applying light and shade and layering glazes to soften the harsh lines.

There was just so much to see that Henry returned the next day. He saw the limitations of former artists, who created new compositions, which had real pictorial space, depth, and subtle feel for the first time.

The following day, Henry spent most of his time looking at Impressionism and post-Impressionism paintings.

How imaginative and inventive were these artists, he thought. There were artworks by Claude Monet, Edgar Degas, Auguste Renoir, Eduard Manet, Camille Pissarro, and paintings by Georges Seurat, Henri de Toulouse Lautrec, Vincent van Gogh, and Paul Cezanne.

He gazed at them for a long time, studying different aspects of each one. Bright colours, thick paint, brushstroke, and subject evolved into Impressionism and post-Impressionism, making this painting style the most popular in modern art. He had completely lost himself in the presence of the masters. He spent a long time observing, learning, and studying these marvelous works. Henry looked at his watch. He had only five minutes to meet up with Ruth to attend a party in their honour at her uncle's home.

The following week they travelled around the countryside; beautiful, picturesque landscapes, manicured gardens, and wildflowers in the fields.

"How enchanting the landscape is!" remarked Ruth. "So different from our bushland."

After spending three weeks in England, they took a ship to Europe. Henry was keen to meet his relatives, and they planned on staying in Hamburg for a few days. He still had some idea of the German language and was fairly confident he would not have problems communicating. At the very least, he would be able to have some interaction with them. Naturally, it was difficult for Ruth. However, they were delighted to see her and soon realised what a fine person she was.

They took a train to Paris to view Toulouse Lautrec's large-scale poster work and visit paintings by the artists from the school of Impressionism. They stayed in Paris for another week, and then caught the ferry back to London after an unforgettable holiday and honeymoon.

Part Three

8

Home Coming

I had already bought an elegant Georgian style, red-painted brick house with an entrance and columns. It belonged to a London businessman, who had bought it intending to spend some time in Tasmania. Unfortunately, he died before he could tread Australian soil.

I had always been partial to the Georgian style of architecture, which defined its elegance, symmetry, and harmony. The English who occupied Van Diemen's Land brought their style of living, dress fashions, eating habits, and architecture, which became part of Australian history. The architects who came initially established Georgian-style homes in their new land. The Australian Georgian houses lacked ornamentation and were usually constructed with a veranda to correspond to the Australian climate.

Our house was a perfect find in a leafy suburb of Hobart, close to my work. Ruth was excited about having her own home. It was a completely new experience for her, but she felt somewhat lost in a new neighbourhood without her family around her. Wynyard was her home. Everyone knew her, always having a friendly smile, cheerful disposition, and an excellent reputation as a teacher.

Parents only heard favourable reports of Ruth.

I realised that it would take her time to adjust to the new environment, and once she found work, she would be fine.

A few days after settling in her new home, there was a knock at the door.

"Hello, Mrs Weston," a woman greeted Ruth with an extended hand. "I am Anne, the neighbour on your left. Welcome to our neighbourhood. I brought you some scones which I just made."

Henry had warned Ruth about Anne. "Be careful with her; she is a gossipmonger and makes it her business to know what goes on in the neighbourhood. She will haunt you."

"How kind of you. Please come in and have a cup of tea."

Anne was delighted to come in and inspect her new neighbour's home. "Do you have friends or family in Hobart, Mrs Weston?"

"Please, call me Ruth. I have an aunt and two cousins who live not far away."

"I think you will like our friendly neighbourhood. We come from the same milieu, and we seem to get on. Some of us have young children, and they play together. I will organise a morning tea soon, and you can get to know them. Would you please call on us if you need any help? We have met your husband. He mentioned he travels to other states from time to time for work. What sort of work does he do?"

"He studied art and design in Melbourne."

"Oh! He is a painter."

"Yes, he is an artist. He has his own company."

"Do you work?"

"I was a primary school teacher in Launceston."

"We have excellent schools in Hobart—more and more children are attending them. You won't have problems finding work. School is only a short walking distance from here, but you don't have to worry about that yet. You only just got married?"

"Yes, only a few weeks ago."

"Where did you go for your honeymoon?"

Ruth did not wish to discuss her honeymoon trip with her.

"How about you, Anne, do you have any children?"

"Yes, we have a boy and a girl. Our daughter is one, and our son is three."

After Ruth said goodbye to Anne, the phone rang.

"Hello, Ruth," Maud said excitedly. There was a chorus of voices in the background greeting her. "How do you like Hobart?"

"I still must get used to it. Henry is going to Melbourne for a while. I think I will come home while he is away."

There was a scream of excitement as Maud told Emily.

The following week, Ruth took a train to Launceston, and from there, the drive to Wynyard would be another couple of hours.

At the mouth of river Ingles, Wynyard was known for its green pastures. Its fertile and agricultural land was most suitable for farming and timber production, exporting timber and dairy, thus becoming a vibrant commercial centre. Its closeness to the river Ingles made exporting goods easier.

Unlike Hobart, Launceston, and the northern region, the government received minimal support, and the area's economic independence came from private enterprise. With the discovery of gold, tin, and other metals in the north, in 1870, Launceston benefitted commercially to a great extent.

Ruth's family met her at the station, and the girls greeted her with screams, hugs, and kisses. Mrs Callaway embraced her daughter with tears in her eyes. She had missed her.

"You have to tell us all the news about the trip, your new home, and Henry," said Emily.

That evening over dinner, Ruth talked, in great detail, about their wonderful time in England and meeting up with the family in London. "Henry's family in Hamburg were very kind to me. They were so happy to see us, and I was amazed how good Henry's German was, despite hardly using the language. I think they were very impressed.

Our cousins are keen on coming to visit us here."

"I can't wait to go overseas and travel and meet up with the relatives in London," said Maud.

"I can't either," said Emily.

"Henry is wonderful. He takes good care of me. His work is much in demand. He also talks about moving to Sydney in a few years and setting up his own business."

The following morning, Ruth went for a walk in the garden. The air was crisp. The dew had settled on the leaves, and the summer flowers, poppies, zinnias, and petunias, were in full bloom. She suddenly realised how much she had missed her home and her family.

She heard sounds coming from the house and made her way to the kitchen. Her father saw her and came out to greet her with a kiss. "Did you sleep well, my dear?"

"Yes, I did."

"I was thinking of taking you all for a drive to the beach following the coastal line. I remember how much you and the girls enjoyed our picnics and the walks in the wilderness, and swimming. Your mother and the girls are getting the picnic lunch ready, and as soon as they are available, we can leave."

The drive through the ancient rainforest on one side and along the beaches with turquoise blue water on the coastal side was captivating. When they reached their favourite picnic area, the girls continued with their natter, with much to catch up on, and the week disappeared too quickly.

How wonderful to be together again, thought Ruth.

"I hope you can come more often," said Emily. "We really miss you."

Ruth came home a day earlier than Henry. She wanted to prepare the meal and have everything ready for him when he returned from his trip. She could not contain her excitement at seeing him.

There was a knock at the door.

Ruth hurriedly went to open the door and was about to greet him, thinking it was Henry when she suddenly stopped and realised that it was Anne.

"Hello, Ruth, I was just checking to see if you are all right."

"Thank you, Anne, I am fine. Henry will be home soon. I thought it was him when I opened the door."

"No matter, if you need anything, I am nearby."

A few minutes later, there was another knock. This time Ruth cautiously opened the door, thinking that it could be Anne again. When she realised it was Henry, she excitedly ran into his arms and he hugged her warmly.

"I missed you, so much," said Ruth.

"I missed you, too," said Henry, and kissed her passionately.

"How was Melbourne?"

"It was good, but busy. I sold a few of my paintings."

"Oh, wonderful," said Ruth.

Henry looked invigorated from his time spent in Melbourne.

"I met up with some of my college friends and artists. Now, with the Impressionist movement in France, Melbourne has become the centre of Australian Impressionism."

"Why is it so different from the colonial period?" asked Ruth, who had very little knowledge of the art world and was eager to learn more. Both sat down on the couch, Ruth with a glass of freshly squeezed orange juice and Henry with a cold beer while Henry explained to Ruth about the current art movement.

"In the history of Tasmania, there was a flourishing art world," explained Henry. "Many artists came from England and Europe and settled in this country. The splendour of the Tasmanian landscapes and the beauty of the seascapes drew artists to this island. When the convicts received their freedom, some took up painting as they settled into their new environment. The British immigrants created most of the colonial art, but they continued to paint English landscapes."

"That is true," said Ruth. "When you think, our sky is unlike the English sky—our light is also different."

"You are so right, Ruth. People still dressed in the manner they did in England. They furnished their homes in the Georgian style; the class distinction was still very prevalent. People surrounded their homes with English gardens and trees."

Ruth listened attentively. "Yes, I agree. Tasmania has a similar climate to England, and the trees found in England grow successfully in our environment."

"However," continued Henry, "people still felt English, and it will take another generation or two for changes to happen."

Ruth got up to check if the roast lamb was ready. Henry moved to the dining room table.

"Oh!" Henry exclaimed, "the table looks absolutely exquisite, Ruth."

She had decorated the table with white and red roses from the garden. The perfume from the flowers was still encircling them. The silver candelabra cast a soft romantic light on the table. She had used the silver cutlery, a wedding gift from Henry's parents.

Henry continued with the conversation. "Melbourne is the most artistic and cultural city in Australia. One reason I studied there was to get into the art school, which the famous Heidelberg artists attended. I was curious to see and visit the areas where the Impressionist artists painted. One weekend, I went to their campsite and spent the entire time with them. It was most inspiring."

"How was Wynyard?" he asked.

"The entire family was so excited to see me. The girls wanted to know all about our trip to England. It was good to be home again, and in a way, it felt like I never left. The garden looked magical with all the colours of the rainbow. They have a new gardener now who is part aboriginal, young and eager to work and learn. I visited some of my friends, and our old haunts with the family. But I missed you and am so glad you are back."

"Let's do something nice on the weekend," Henry suggested.

"How about horse riding?"

"That sounds wonderful."

"I have received the wedding photos, which we can look through at the weekend as well."

"Oh! Very good," said Henry. They were both looking forward to spending time together.

9

Ruth's Decision

Having settled into her home, Ruth considered teaching or joining a charitable organisation and helping the needy. She spoke to one of her neighbours who was working for the Anglican Church in Hobart.

"We need people at the shed. We have just started distributing food and clothing to a small aboriginal village, where people live in deplorable conditions."

The Tasmanian Aborigines became cut off from the Australian mainland because of the rising sea level. By the 19th century, most Aborigines died because of diseases, and constant warfare with the British. A small group of Aborigines survived who had settled near Hobart. As time went on, they moved closer to Hobart, searching for food, being hunters and gatherers. They established themselves in a fertile area near to river Derwent.

"I would be interested in something like that," said Ruth.

She went and discussed her idea with Henry.

"It is a great idea, an excellent service; it is something that would suit your caring and giving nature." Ruth was happy with Henry's encouragement.

The following week, she went with Elizabeth to see the supervisor who explained her task to Ruth. "You would have to take the goods to the village with a driver on a horse and buggy.

"The first day will be for sorting out the clothing that would be suitable for the children, and pack them in a bag, with two separate bags for the adults. The next day you will need to do the shopping and buy some food for them."

"What do they eat?"

"They have their food, such as yams, and other tubers and a variety of bush potatoes, which women dig out of the ground, as well as insects, ants, grubs, and moths. The sea provides them with fish, turtles, eels, whatever they can get. We take bread, fruit seeds and nuts, and sometimes biscuits."

Once Ruth got all the food and clothing together, Jimmy, the driver, loaded them onto the carriage, and they rode for half an hour before they caught sight of the camp.

As they drew nearer, they could hear the children's sounds, and suddenly they were running and waving towards them.

As soon as they heard the buggy, the children knew that they had visitors. Ruth greeted them with a smile. "Hello, how are you?"

They did not understand and started giggling. Ruth laughed with them. They all surrounded her, and some were touching her.

Ruth took the food to the head of the village. He thanked her; he had some knowledge of English and had spent some time working on a farm. On the way home, she thought about the children, who had no education, very little hygiene knowledge, and no western medicine.

She found out that the Aborigines had been using natural plants for generations. Aboriginal culture, which uses bush medicines and the healing environment, was linked with their spiritual world. A healer in the aboriginal society acted as an intermediary between the sick and the spiritual world.

The medicine man prescribed herbs and other remedies while performing spiritual rituals. It was not always easy to find such medicine. They travelled many days to locate the plants and trees needed to produce the medication. Some plants were not available because of the seasonal changes.

After a few months of visiting the campsite and getting to know the people, she thought she could use her knowledge as a teacher and teach the children. She got in touch with the education department and received permission to spend some time in the village and introduce some basic English. The elder of the tribe consented. The education department provided her with a blackboard.

On the day she started, she gathered the children together with the elder's help, who explained Ruth's intentions and asked them to sit on the ground and listen carefully to what she said. Ruth produced some pictures of fruit and items she had brought to the camp and related the words to the images. When the children became familiar with the terms, Ruth made basic sentences with a few words. Once they had mastered the introductory sentences, she slowly introduced the alphabet. She continued this process for about 12 months until the children could understand some basic sentences. The camp elder, who stood at a distance, watched and was also eager to learn. The children enjoyed the process and accepted Ruth as a friend.

Twelve months later, Ruth went to the Education Department and came up with a proposal to establish a school for the parents and children at the campsite. After investigating the camp, they erected a rudiment timber enclosure. They provided another teacher who could instruct husbands and wives as well.

10

Adoption

Two years had passed since Ruth moved to Hobart and set up her home. She had created a garden of splendour, and it was all-consuming for her. It became her child. A child she had been yearning for since she had been married. Her effort to conceive for the last two years had failed. After three miscarriages, her doctor had discouraged her from trying again.

"I realise conception is not an effortless task for you, and perhaps, if you are desperate for a child, then you should adopt one. Many babies are waiting for a mother to love and care for them."

On her way home, she thought about adoption. It might be the way to go. At least they would love the child and give them a life they may not have had.

When Henry returned, she explained to him what the doctor had said. Henry knew that Ruth desperately wanted a child.

"How do you feel about it?" Henry asked.

"I think I would like to adopt a girl, if that is fine with you."

It was not a simple task, Ruth realised. She rang her mother first to discuss the situation.

"Ruth, are you sure that's what you want to do?"

"Yes, I am."

"It won't be easy, Ruth. We know nothing about her pedigree, her background, and what the future will bring. Think about it before you decide."

Mrs Callaway went and spoke to her husband about it.

"She shouldn't," he remarked. "She should go back to teaching; there are plenty of children at school, she could enjoy spending time with."

Mrs Callaway knew it wasn't the same but refrained from verbalising her thoughts.

Ruth realised from her research that the decision to adopt a child could be fraught with problems. There was a stigma attached to unwed mothers. Society ostracised them, as they brought disgrace to their families. For the parents, it was an equally complex problem. They often sent their daughters to rural areas to have the baby, and they directly placed them for adoption.

Society's attitude towards infertility was also negative, and a cause for gossip and rumours. Mothers suffered from detachment. Because of the high infant mortality and infanticide cases in 1896, the parliament enacted the Children's Acts legislation.

Legally, adoption was a confidential, irrevocable process where 'unwanted' babies were placed predominantly with childless couples, relieving the State from the burden of their care. Since they enacted the first Australian legislation facilitating adoption, thousands of children had been given up for adoption.

The following week, Ruth started making some enquiries regarding the orphanages where they fostered children. Ruth was volunteering at the Anglican Church. She met Rose there, and their friendship developed. She invited her for afternoon tea and told her about her intention of adopting a child.

"Do you have any idea what the best place is to visit?"

"The one run by the Anglican Church in South Hobart has an excellent reputation. It is a rescue home for single mothers from where the babies are adopted.

The church's idea, along with other authorities behind the rescue home, was to change the women's promiscuous behaviour."

"A little harsh," said Ruth. "I am sure all of them are not promiscuous. It must be hard for young girls when they fall in love and are too young to realise the consequence of their action."

"I know the wife of the bishop of Tasmania has pushed to establish this home. Many women become pregnant out of wedlock. Some were thrown out of their homes because they were poor and could not feed another mouth. The bishop's wife is very involved in training mothers for work, so that when they leave, they can find a job. The home also employs women to encourage them in work ethic. They work in the laundry and do the ironing. Sometimes the mothers take their babies home. If you like, I will talk to Bertha about your intention to adopt a child."

Ruth found out that the Home of Mercy was founded in 1890 and run by the Church. Originally it was a reform home for women. Later it became a large organisation, incorporating various branches, admitting children from all parts of the State, often for a short period until the new parents could take them home. Sometimes, if the mother had more children at home and had difficulty looking after them, she would leave her infant at the Home of Mercy until she could care for the baby. They adopted out many unwanted babies.

The following week, Ruth received an invitation to visit the hospital, to discuss the adoption process that Rose had organised with Bertha. She was both nervous and anxious. Henry was in Melbourne again, to sell some of his work. As soon as Ruth met Bertha, she instantly felt at ease, and all her nervousness vanished. She spoke to her about her desire to have children, her miscarriages and her doctor's recommendation for adoption.

"There is a child," said Bertha, "whose mother died in childbirth. She is 18 months old now. If you are interested, I can take you to the cottage where the mothers with children stay until they are ready to go home. In the meantime, they are trained in various skills so that it would be easier for them to find jobs enabling them to support themselves."

Bertha took Ruth to the cottage. The large room they entered was noticeably clean and tidy. It was a recreation area where mothers could compare notes, and the children could play. She saw how young the mothers looked.

"There is Lizzie," said Bertha, pointing to a little blonde-haired girl who was sitting away from the rest of the children and observing them. Bertha went over to her. "Hello, Lizzie." She looked at Bertha and smiled. "Come here." She picked her up and introduced her to Ruth.

"Hello," Ruth said with a big smile on her face as she started playing with her and chatting to her. Lizzie kept her eyes on her and then suddenly smiled.

"We have to go now, Lizzie," said Bertha, putting her on the floor. She cried when one of the other mothers came over and took her to play with her daughter.

As soon as Ruth returned home, she rang her mother.

"Mum, I think I have found an adorable girl. I would like to adopt her."

"What does Henry think?" she asked, somewhat irritated.

"He has left it completely to me. His opinion is that I am the one who will raise the child, and it is important for me to be happy with what I am doing."

"All right," said Mrs Callaway, "I will catch the train on Monday."

Ruth was both excited and terrified. She needed her Mother's help to come to some sort of decision. "Am I doing the right thing?" she thought. "It is a risk I am taking, and what if it doesn't work out?" All these thoughts were racing through her head.

When Henry got home from work, he noticed her face looking tired.

"Are you all right, Ruth?"

She exploded with the news, her interview with Bertha, seeing Lizzie, and her mother coming on Monday to help her out.

"Ruth, first, you need to calm down. You have time to think about the consequences of adopting a child. If you feel you are doing the right thing, then go ahead with it. No need to rush, you have plenty of time."

Ruth met her mother at the train station. The following day, she took her mother to the home, to get to know Lizzie a little better.

At first, Mrs Callaway was very reserved, wondering if Ruth was doing the right thing.

After a while, she noticed that she immediately felt comfortable with Ruth, every time they came to visit Lizzie.

A month later, Ruth signed the adoption papers and took Lizzie home. Henry was waiting to greet them. Ruth's mother stayed with them for two weeks to help her daughter care for Lizzie. It was the beginning of a new life for Ruth.

Lizzie was a crucial priority in her life. After all, is it not a mother's duty to nurture a child and provide for her needs?

It turned out that Lizzie was not an easy baby. She often woke up screaming in the middle of the night, and nothing would settle her down until, tired from crying, she went to sleep. Henry was away a lot, establishing his name in Melbourne and Sydney. During these times, Mrs Callaway came and stayed with Ruth.

As she grew up, Lizzie was an unusual child. She suffered from nightmares and woke up screaming. Finally, Ruth spoke to the orphanage about Lizzie's behaviour and wanted to know about her background.

"We have little information about her, except that she was an unwanted child. Her mother took her own life because of the abuse she suffered from her husband. The police had questioned Lizzie's father regarding the bruises his wife had as well as the child. The court found him guilty of abusing both mother and child. He was charged and went to prison for six months."

Ruth continued trying to become pregnant, and three years later, she did, against her doctor's wishes. Ruth and Henry were delighted. It was a moment she had been anxiously waiting for, and it finally came. They had a son. But soon, joy turned to sadness. The doctors realised the child had severe issues. His breathing was slow, and he was severely handicapped. The doctors warned Ruth that he could die. But Charles did survive. Ruth had the choice of leaving him in an institution or taking him home.

"There is no way I will place my child in an institution. Only if I can't manage him, maybe. I have read about mental institutions, and they don't treat patients well. I don't want my child to suffer," she said tearfully.

Both Ruth and Henry brought Charles home after three weeks. Mrs Callaway was there to help Lizzie in those difficult circumstances. Ruth struggled to do the best for her child. In the end, it became impossible. He grew, and he became heavier to lift and transport from one place to another. By the time he was four, she could not manage his needs. Ruth was looking tired from lack of sleep and had lost much weight.

"Look at you, Ruth. You look like a waif. You are half the size of what you used to be. You can't do this any longer."

"Charlie should be in a home. The Home of Mercy is close to us—it has an excellent reputation. The nuns will take good care of him. I will make the necessary arrangements."

"I heard and read about how the mentally ill patients in the institutions received treatment during the convict period. When the first fleet arrived in Australia, the ship brought mentally ill convicts and criminals, who were thrown together in the same goal at Parramatta. The governor and the military regime controlled the penal system of the colony. They decided on the treatment of demented human beings.

"Later, they established asylums when they realised that all the imprisoned convicts were not criminals but were mentally ill patients. Still, the treatment of them continued to be harsh. They imprisoned young and old behind the asylum walls."

"Ruth, it is not like that anymore. There are places particularly for children, and they are well looked after."

"Even though," Ruth continued, "not everyone was damaged to the same degree, they were all treated cruelly, chained to posts in their vomit, urine, and often starved for misbehaving.

"How can human beings be so cruel? They were under the power of the wardens, who could deal with them in whatever way they thought right."

"Ruth, it is true the orphanages were known for their dehumanized treatments of children. Untrained wardens took care of disabled people. The severely handicapped individuals did not have a long life: In the later years, the State and churches constructed institutions to house them. The nurses and the wardens receive training now. In the past, they did not have the proper knowledge. Past is past, Ruth. Things have changed."

"You don't need training to be caring," said Ruth.

11

Lizzie

"Lizzie," called her mother from the kitchen, "are you ready for school yet?" There was no reply.

"Lizzie," called Ruth again, with a slightly raised voice. Still no answer. "Lizzie," she raised her voice with exasperation, one octave higher than before.

"I am not feeling well. I have a headache," replied Lizzie with annoyance.

"Come on, Lizzie, we will be late."

Lizzie did not stir. She was dressed in her school uniform, sat on her bed, clutching her doll. It was a gift from her grandmother, which she treasured and found solace in whenever she was sad or upset. It helped to soothe her anxiety.

Just then, the phone rang.

"Hello Mrs Weston; this is Home of Mercy calling. Charles is not well; he has a temperature. We have given him some tablets to bring his fever down, but he is very restless."

"I will be there soon," Ruth responded with concern.

First, she had to sort Lizzie, who was still in her room. Lizzie's performance was a regular occurrence, a drama

Ruth could do without this morning. Finally, Ruth went into Lizzie's room with her lunch, put it inside her school bag, took her hand and rushed outside.

"The tram will be here any minute now."

They hurriedly caught the tram. Ten minutes later, it stopped at the station opposite the school.

"Goodbye, Lizzie," Ruth called out, "see you this afternoon."

Lizzie got up and walked off.

As usual, she was not looking forward to going to school. Unlike the girls who attended classes with laughter and chatter, she had no desire to be there. Lizzie could not mingle with her classmates, join in their conversations, or play games with them. She found it challenging to make friends, and if she made a friend, it was only for a brief period.

Lizzie's behaviour was not conducive to a lasting friendship. She was a disturbance in the class, always looking for attention. Often, she would look around the room and pull funny faces, causing suppressed giggles from classmates. She preferred her own company during class breaks and rebelled against any discipline. Ruth felt disquieted by Lizzie's lack of interest in her school activities and her behaviour at home.

It took her another half an hour before she reached Mercy's Home. She sat erect, with her hair in a bun, gazing outside, absorbed in her thoughts. Ruth was not a great beauty, but her charm lay in her demeanour. She carried herself with confidence and displayed sparkling brown eyes and a radiant smile.

When she arrived at the Home of Mercy, she knocked on a large, overpowering gate, in heavy timber, bolted from inside. The matron, a portly woman with a stern face, opened the door.

"Mrs Weston, you are early. We have a set time for visits. Charles is not ready yet. Please wait outside until he is prepared."

Ruth had not met the new matron before. "What an unfriendly person," she thought. "Do we need people like this running a children's home?" She sat down reluctantly on an old uncomfortable metal chair on the veranda and waited impatiently to see her son.

It was a bright spring morning. The sun glistened and shed a translucent light on the bark of the grey gum tree. She cast her eyes around her and observed the splendour of the neatly manicured garden. Spring flowers raised their heads in vibrant pinks, reds, and yellows. Bleeding hearts, heart-shaped in the colours of pink, white, and red, dangled charmingly in the shade across the length of its branches.

A wren dressed in a fanciful light, dark blue and grey costume gracefully made ballerina leap from one bough to another. The merry sound of birds chirping and springing from one flower to another was music to her ears. But within her, the noise was deafening.

Ruth felt guilty about leaving Charles in a home. There was a stigma attached to mentally incapacitated people—classed as lunatics, unhealthy, and deviants of the society—and they were isolated, housed on the city's outskirts. Their behaviour was regarded as aberrant, a possible risk to the community, and fostered by society's attitude towards the isolated living style, which further stigmatised them. They suffered from neglect, treated cruelly by staff and matrons. The predominant attitude towards disability was that individuals who were incapable of contributing to society had to rely on welfare and charitable organisations.

In the past, in certain societies, mental illness was regarded as being possessed by evil spirits and demons. The possessor had to go through certain rituals and undertakings, administered under a priest or a religious person or one who had the power of driving the spirit out of a ravaged body. Such was the case in the Old Testament or the Jewish Torah or Hindu belief. In Christian texts, Jesus had been casting devils out of the bodies, and Mary Magdalene was one such person. The first person who could diagnose mental illness in terms of disorder of physiology was a Greek physician in 400 BC.

Before the 1900s, people in Tasmania who had mental illnesses, such as mental defects, epilepsy, autism, and cerebral palsy, lived at home, and families took care of them. Life expectancy for significantly disabled children was not a long one. In the early 1900s, the state government and local administrative agencies built institutions to house people with disabilities and trained male and female staff to work.

The parents of disabled children also suffered humiliation, isolation, and depression. Their mothers found it difficult to manage them at home. Poverty, other children to feed and take care of, and the scorn of abusive husbands were determinants for leaving the children in institutions. Later, the government introduced state psychologists and clinics to diagnose both children and adults. Children with behavioural problems, disadvantaged due to abuse, poverty, neglected upbringing, and deafness, were all classed under mental deficiency.

"Mrs Weston," said a loud voice, making Ruth shudder and bringing her back to the present. "You can see your son now. Follow me, please."

They both walked silently along a dark and uninviting corridor, with loud noises coming from both directions until they reached the infirmary.

"My Charles," she said in dismay.

Charles was lying in bed with his tongue hanging out, eyes rolling around and mumbling incoherently. She came over and sat near him and leaned over to caress him.

"Charlie," she whispered, "mummy is here."

At once, he looked at his mother and gave her a beaming smile. Charlie's voice had been taken away from him since birth, but his smile and eyes became his voice. She stayed with him for a good while, cuddling him. She talked to him about his father, his work, and about the painting he had just sold.

"Lizzie sends her love." Charles did not know what his mother was telling him, but he loved to hear her voice.

Often when she visited Charlie, she took a picture book with her and read to him. He loved looking at the pictures, especially of animals. Every time he saw elephants or monkeys, and the tall giraffes, he would laugh and mumble something. When Charlie went to sleep, Ruth took her book out of the bag and read. She was a keen reader, and she would find comfort in her books during hard times.

When she returned home, she brewed a cup of tea, went outside, and sat on the veranda. Charles was six and had been in the home for two years. It was difficult for Ruth to take care of him. He was both mentally and physically disabled. He needed 24-hour care, which she found difficult to maintain. She had to deal with her daughter's tantrums. She realised Lizzie felt neglected, and her behaviour had worsened.

Charlie was an enigma to Henry. When Charlie was still at home, Henry did not know how to handle him. Occasionally, at Ruth's request, Henry would pick him up and take him outside. When Henry was home, she had to attend to his needs. Ruth found it very challenging to take care of everyone; it took a heavy toll on her health.

She took another sip and called her mother.

"I wasn't expecting to hear from you today. Is everything all right?" asked her mother. She was surprised to hear from Ruth as they had spoken only two days ago.

"You sound downhearted. I had a feeling all was not well with you. How is Charlies?" she enquired.

"Charlie is unwell. He is running a high temperature, and the nurses took him to the infirmary. He was happy to see me. Henry is thinking about moving to Sydney to expand his career. The art movement in Sydney is developing and becoming the centre of Australia. Well-known artists and emerging artists are taking part in the Impressionist movement."

Mrs Callaway did not know what the Impressionist movement was. She thought it must be something to do with Henry's line of work.

"What will happen to Charlie?" her mother remarked.

"I won't be able to visit him as often as I do now."

Mrs Callaway listened to this news with surprise.

"But he has a good job here and is so well-known in his field."

"Nothing is decided yet," said Ruth.

When they had finished their conversation, she went to the kitchen, made a sandwich, and returned to her chair. The sun was still warm and pleasant, a gentle breeze was blowing, and she could smell the rosemary and lavender in her garden. The thought of leaving Charlie was haunting her. "At the very least, my mother will visit him and take care of him and keep me informed. It's some consolation," she thought.

She cast a wistful eye at her garden, which she had created and put her spirit into. It was a labour of love. It became her lover, her passion, her saviour, and an escape from the chagrins of her life.

When she first moved into the property, it looked as if it was laid to rest. Decaying leaves, branches, fallen trees, and overgrown weeds lay unkempt. Only a patch of rough grass, a meagre box hedge, and a few ancient trees scattered around the property survived.

She read gardening magazines, which displayed historical gardens in Europe, and drew ideas from them. Ruth used Buxus for hedges. Planted purple hydrangeas, blue and white irises, and foxgloves bloomed in season. Perfume from red, white, and pink roses permeated the air. She went over and picked a few and took them inside to arrange them on the table. She returned to her seat outside with her gardening magazine, which she was reading, and sat down to continue where she had left off.

Lizzie, as usual, walked home from school. She went straight into her room, threw her bag on the floor, and lay on her bed.

"Lizzie," her mother called out after a few minutes, "come and have something to eat. I made your favourite cookies."

After a few minutes, Lizzie appeared and joined her. She sat silently munching cookies and obliviously gazing outside.

"How was your day?" Ruth inquired.

"Awful," said Lizzie. "The sports teacher was picking on me all the time while the rest of the girls were misbehaving. It wasn't fair."

Lizzie looked up at her mother. "What's wrong with you? You don't look so well."

"Your father is thinking of moving to Sydney because of his work."

"Why do we have to move to Sydney? And what about Charlie?"

"Charlie will remain in the hospital until we find a new place for him. Or, we might have to leave him behind."

"What about Grandma?"

"Grandma will come and stay with us in Sydney from time to time. But everything is uncertain. Papa hasn't made any decisions yet."

"All the work that you have put into this garden—what will happen with it?"

Ruth was surprised, and at the same time, pleased to hear Lizzie's comments.

She had just finished cooking when Henry arrived home. She did not hear him opening the front door until he called out, "I'm home!"

"You are early today," she remarked.

"I have finished my project and decided to come home to see how it went with Lizzie." Sadly, she thought, Henry was more concerned about Lizzie's reaction than his son, Charlie's.

"How did Lizzie take the news of moving to Sydney?"

"Not well. Lizzie does not adjust to change quickly, as you know. She is in her room, most likely mulling over moving to Sydney. I feel we should wait a couple more years. Lizzie will be older, and I don't think I can leave Charles behind just yet."

"Lizzie," called out her father, "dinner is ready."

She came, hugged her dad, and sat down for dinner.

"How about going riding tomorrow?" Lizzie's eyes brightened up, and her whole demeanour changed.

"Yes," she nodded.

Henry introduced riding to Lizzie at an early age. Since then, she enjoyed it and loved horses—a good outlet for calming her down. He hired two horses for the day, and both rode through the countryside. Sometimes she raced off, whipping the horse to go as fast as it could. Sometimes she imagined herself flying and being free.

She was attached to her father, who never remonstrated her behaviour. That was a mother's task, he believed. She always returned home relaxed and satisfied. Henry pondered moving to Sydney. In the end, he decided to wait for another two years until Lizzie was old enough to start secondary school. Instead, he would spend some time in Sydney, familiarise himself with the place and people, exhibit his work from time to time, and look for land to design and build a home.

12

Two Months Later

On his way home, Henry checked his letterbox. It had become a habit, even though Ruth or Lizzie always did. This time, to his surprise, he found a letter from the Bulletin.

Dear Henry Weston,
We would like to offer you a job at the Bulletin magazine to work with Norman Lindsay in the design and illustration section. We have read your credentials, and if possible, we would like to see you and discuss the matter in person. If all goes well, you can start next month.

Henry, of course, was thrilled with the offer. He remembered Norman from his student days and working with him in Melbourne. They were also part of the Bohemian Sketch Club. The move to Sydney and working for the Bulletin was something he wanted to be involved in, but he would have to discuss this with Ruth and Lizzie, and he also has Charles to consider.

The next day at work, he wrote back.

Dear Sir,

Thank you for your letter and your work offer with Norman Lindsay as an illustrator. I met Norman in Melbourne in my student days, and it would be a pleasure to work with him. Next week, I will be in Sydney to exhibit my paintings at the Art Society, and I look forward to meeting you and discussing your offer.

Yours sincerely
Henry Weston

"I have some good news to tell you both," said Henry, unsure of the reaction, especially from Lizzie.

"I had a letter from the Bulletin in Sydney, offering me a chance to work in their Sydney office. They are allowing me to work with Norman Lindsay. I had a lot to do with Norman in my student days, and we got on very well. It is an honour to be invited to be part of the Bulletin."

"That's wonderful news," said Ruth. "It's something you always wanted."

"I don't want to go to Sydney," said Lizzie. "I like it here, and I will miss my friends."

"I thought you didn't have any friends?" remarked Ruth

"That's not true; I have two friends; we are in the same sports team."

"I am sure you will make friends in Sydney," said Henry. "

My work is essential, and to make any progress, I would have to move to Sydney. Eventually, I am keen to open my own company. Working for the Bulletin would be the first step in that direction."

"If you don't wish to move straight away, I have a suggestion," he continued, facing Ruth. "I will move to Sydney and start work. You stay behind, and when Lizzie finishes primary school in two years, she can attend secondary school in Sydney. I will come and visit you from time to time, and you can visit me in Sydney. I am sure your mother won't mind staying with you and helping you. Now that Emily and Maud are studying in Hobart, she can see them more often. I think you will like Sydney."

"Yes," said Ruth, "that is a possibility."

"We can visit you in the holidays," said Lizzie, adopting a cheerful demeanour.

The following day, before Ruth could leave the house, there was a phone call from Maud.

"Hello Ruth," she said, and burst out crying. She could not utter a word.

"What is the matter, Maud? Why are you so upset?"

"I am afraid I have some bad news for you. Our dad had a massive heart attack last night, and he died instantly."

"I will catch the next train to Wynyard," said Ruth, trying not to burst into tears.

Tearfully, she rang Henry and told him.

"I am coming home now and will take you to the station. I am making some travel inquiries before I leave."

Henry arrived two hours later. He took her into his arms.

"I am so sorry, Ruth; I know how close you are to your father. The train is leaving at 2 p.m. I can pick up Lizzie from school, and we will take the train tomorrow."

The following day, when they arrived in Wynyard, he quickly took over the funeral arrangements with the girls and Mrs Callaway. After the massive funeral, they held a wake in the town hall; practically the entire town was present. Henry returned to work, and Ruth, Lizzie, and the sisters stayed behind to help sort out their mother's immediate needs.

A few days after the funeral, the family sat on the veranda, resting and trying to take in the reality of what had just happened, feeling the loss of their outstanding and loving father.

Friends kept coming, bringing food and homemade cakes and biscuits. All the family needed at this point was quiet, reflective time on their own.

"Mum, what are you going to do without Dad around? It is a large farm; how will you manage? You have not been very involved with the business side of it," said Ruth.

"Yes, dear Ruth, I have been thinking about this quite a lot. I will have to sell the property and get a smaller place."

"I have an idea," said Ruth. "Why don't you move to Hobart? You will be closer to us. Now that the girls are studying and working in Hobart, they plan to stay there, or, perhaps, travel. We will move to Sydney in a couple of years. You could move into our house, and eventually, when we have our house in Sydney, you can buy it from us. The girls can come and stay there, and it will be like old times again, except without Dad."

Suddenly, at the mention of their father, tears came rolling down their cheeks.

Lizzie was thrilled. "Oh! Grandma," she exclaimed, "what a brilliant idea. We could do many things together when we visit you, and as well when you come to Sydney."

Mrs Callaway smiled, wiping her tears. Lizzie went over and sat on her grandma's lap, cuddling her.

After two weeks with her mother, Ruth left with Lizzie and, a week later, Henry travelled to Sydney for his art exhibition and an interview with Archibald. His paintings sold well, and he accepted the job with the Bulletin.

Part Four

13

The Bulletin

In 1888, J F Archibald and John Haynes founded the Bulletin magazine. Its attitude was revolutionary. Its aim was not to cater to the 'polite society' but to the readers who lived in the bush. The Bulletin opened a whole new world to readers in the country and tried to unify Australians with its down-to-earth approach. The Australian environment was inherently different from the English. The pattern of life, climate, and classless society contributed to the Australian characteristics and qualities, especially in the bush.

In its early days, the Bulletin's contents proved to be controversial. It promoted Australia for the white man, disregarding its original inhabitants and the many immigrants who had come to Australia. It was radical in its style, anti-English, and anti-royalist, and it included racist cartoons and sexist articles.

The Bulletin became the most popular magazine on the newsstand. With a weekly circulation of 80,000 copies, it became the bible for the bushman, uniting the cities throughout Australia with the country.

It promoted uniquely Australian writings, using Australian idioms, Australian words in bush ballads, bush poetry, stories from all walks of life, and portrayed the romantic view of life in the country. It was also labour-orientated and supported its campaigns. However, it was becoming disenchanted with Prime Minister Robert Hughes's directions and the NSW premier's spending habits. They stopped supporting their efforts but continued promoting their aspirations.

Between 1885 and 1901, the Australian Federation's formation caused many social and economic changes. The improvements in general, communications, and rail links aided in uniting this massive country.

The country's population was increasing, and sixty per cent of the people were born in Australia. At the same time, the country was experiencing droughts. The money market had collapsed, followed by economic depression and the rise of the trade union movement. The Bulletin was becoming politically conscious of the many changes to Australian society.

Women were vocalising their right to vote, the labour movement was becoming intense, and Australia was slowly establishing its own identity. A cultural change was also happening in all areas of the arts. There was a rise of nationalist sentiments, and the writers such as Henry Lawson and Banjo Paterson used the Bulletin magazine's medium in promoting the bush. They created the bushman's idea as the real Australians, written from an Australian perspective, with a larrikin spirit of society, politics, and events.

A poem by Henry Lawson, 'A Prouder Man Than You' gives a pertinent description of a country person and a city slicker:

If you fancy that your people came of better stock than mine,
If you hint of higher breeding by a word or by a sign,
If you're proud because of fortune or the clever things you do—
Then I'll play no second fiddle: I'm a prouder man than you!

If you think that your profession has the more gentility,
And that you are condescending to be seen along with me.
If you notice that I'm shabby while your clothes
are spruce and new
You have only got to hint it: I'm a prouder man than you!

Under Archibald, the Bulletin established careers for many Australians. The focus was on Australian materials such as stories and illustrations.

Prominent literary and artistic figures were Henry Lawson, Banjo Paterson Miles Franklin, and Edwin Henry, known as Breaker Morant. Archibald became a patron of Australian arts during his lifetime and later established the Archibald Portrait Prize.

In 1883, a well-established New York cartoonist, Hopkins left America for Australia on a three-year contract to work for the Bulletin but stayed for life. He brought a photo processing engraving machine, replacing the woodblock, which took away the tedious engraving process from the hand engravers. Hopkins, known as Hop, had a dry, laconic humour, making him an instant success with those who surrounded him. Hop became Australia's best-known cartoonist, who produced approximately 19,000 drawings for the journal.

In the 1880s and 1890s, Australia had many similarities with Hopkins' place of origin, a pioneering society, somewhat free from class distinctions. However, the labour movement was beginning to be threatened by a new republican sentiment.

Macleod and Hopkins,1884, published in the Bulletin, 1884

In May 1901, Archibald employed Norman Lindsay as a staff artist, producing cartoons, decorations, and illustrations for jokes and stories for the Bulletin. Norman had no hesitation in accepting it for an offer of 6 pounds a week. In Melbourne, he worked with Lionel, a talented artist, on illustrations and drawings for caricatures, images, and pictures for a weekly magazine. Norman Lindsay was an incredibly talented man, and in some ways, he was a man before his times. He created nudes and mythological characters, which people did not appreciate. He created a repertoire of works that included etchings, drawings, watercolours, woodcuts, bookplates, and lithographs. Norman also wrote novels and children's books such as 'The Magic Pudding.' He also made furniture, carved frames, and surrounded his home with sculptures.

Lindsay was against the war's futility, death, destruction, and the suffering it caused humanity. As Bertolt Brecht once said regarding the great war:

"Seem as inevitable as the power of nature, but whereas earth tremors come to an end, man's inhumanity to man never seems to end."

Norman Lindsay presented a political view of the war through his cartoons and illustrations. At the same time, he agitated nationalistic feelings in young Australians, to enrol in the army and fight for their country and civilisation. The Bulletin changed its leanings from its left orientation to a more right-wing political view.

The Alternative 29 November 1917.
'It's no use, old girl. If he won't go and the country won't send him, I must do it.'
Bulletin cartoon

Bulletin cartoon. 29 November,1917, Norman Lindsay

I had already met Norman Lindsay at the students' club in the Prehistoric Order of the Cannibals. I found him very personable. I had noticed his remarkable blue eyes, that were always in motion, and his hands, which appeared very sensitive. We had lost contact, both going our separate ways. It pleased us to see each other again.

Lindsay showed me the work that he was doing and his illustration style. He invited me to the pub to reacquaint ourselves with each other's lives from our Melbourne student days.

"After you left," said Norman, "I remained in Melbourne for a while and was able to get a job with my brother Lionel in a local magazine. Then, I was invited by Archibald to join the Bulletin magazine. For a while, I left the Bulletin and travelled to Europe in 1909 and produced 101 sketches for Petronius' book, called 'Satyr Icon.' You probably haven't heard of Petronius; he was a Roman courtier during Nero's period. When I returned, I went back to work for the Bulletin magazine. Then, with my wife Rose, we travelled to England, and I spent some time in the museum in South Kensington, where I immersed myself in drawing model ships, which essentially stimulated my interest in ships."

"What an interesting life you have had!" I said.

"Why don't you come and spend next weekend at my property in Springwood? I usually travel to Springwood during the weekends, where I work on my other projects."

"Why did you choose to live so far away from the city?"

"Well, I was not in good health when I was in Melbourne and suffered from pleurisy, so when I returned to Sydney, I decided to move to Leura, for its temperate weather, and fresher air which is good for my lungs. I love the forest. I take beautiful walks, inhale the clean, fresh air and smell the perfumes surrounding me."

The following Saturday, I caught the train to Springwood for the first time. Eucalyptus trees lined the landscape and gave the area a blue colouring. Through the forest, I could see the Blue Mountains at a distance. It was a beautiful spring morning; the air was refreshing and invigorating, and the sun was gently appearing.

Norman picked me up at the station and took me for a brief drive to get acquainted with the town and its environs.

"This town reminds me of Hobart, where I live. It looks quaint and cosy. How did you come across this beautiful property?"

"One day I was riding down woodcutters' track. I saw a sign with 17 hectares of land for sale, with a stone house for 500 pounds. So, I bought it immediately. We had some major renovations done and established a garden with lots of statues. I often have parties with artists and writers travelling from Sydney who stay overnight, or all weekend."

"I seem to have gained a reputation for having wild parties," he said with a mischievous smile. "I will invite you to the next one. You can see for yourself. Come next weekend and spend it with us, and I will give you a tour of our beautiful surroundings."

After I settled into my room, Norman came to take me to his studio, which he had changed significantly over a period. It was a sizeable, detached area from the main house, with a massive table placed in a position considering the importance of light: books, his artworks, and memorabilia cluttered his studio.

"I have not managed to organise the room yet; I have only just moved in." Norman was very enthusiastic about showing me his nude sketches.

"Your sketches and portraits are very unusual. With one single stroke of the pen, your ability to capture an expression is impressive," I remarked.

"I love sketching nudes," said Norman. "I used to draw them from a very early age. My mother confined me indoors until the age of six because of a blood disorder, which caused rashes and blisters on my skin. Because of that, she forbade me to perform any physical activity. So, I spent my time drawing from anything I could get hold of, magazines, journals, or anything in the house. Unfortunately, my mother's puritan values prevented me from drawing what I wanted.

"When I was older, I was allowed to sit at my sister's and friends' drawing classes given by a governess. I used to secretly tear sheets of paper from exercise books and draw human forms. Drawing and sketching became an obsession with me."

"Lindsay was also an intellectual. He read a lot like me, and we communicated on a similar level. We both had read Nietzsche, which profoundly influenced Norman's life. I, like Norman, rejected the views of Christianity. He liked the following lines from Nietzsche:

"You have your way. I have my way. As for the right way, the correct way, and the only way, it does not exist."

Norman Lindsay used myths and legends from the classical period to create his art. He was a more romantic painter, and Ruben's art of painting influenced him.

Norman was ahead of his time in sketching nudes, which created much controversy during his era.

As a cartoonist, painter, commercial artist, and architect with my credentials, I was an asset to the Bulletin magazine, with a successful poster and advertising career in Melbourne. I produced various cartoon subjects for the Bulletin, such as the old salts and waterfront characters.

I skillfully created three provoking posters with captions:

"Yes or no, which?" "Fancy not wantin' to go, Bill!", and "Liberty or slavery, you must choose!"

The idea behind these vibrant posters was to make young men feel pride for their country. The way to do this was to enlist in the army and fight for it. After the war, I said that my maxim was Australian posters for the Australian people. I used the imagery of bushfires and sport to show this idea.

I enjoyed working with Norman, Hop, and other artists at the Bulletin. It prepared me for my future aspirations.

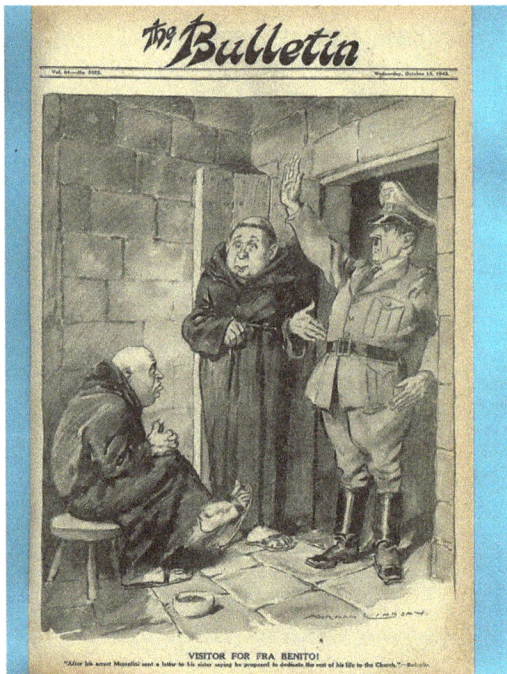

Bulletin Cartoon, 1917, Visitor for Fra Benito, Norman Lindsay

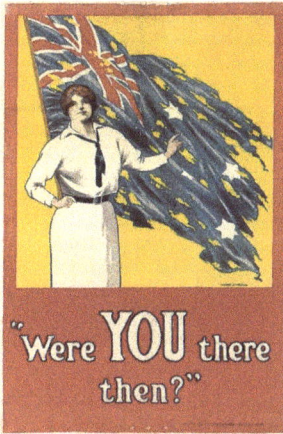

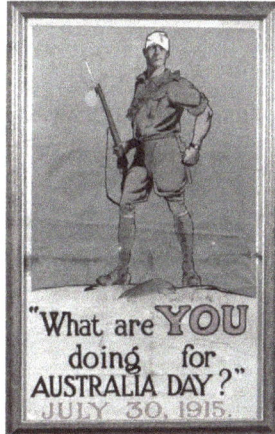

Posters designed by Harry Weston for The Bulletin, 1915-17

14

Edwards Beach

"Other artists paint a bridge, a house, a boat, and that's the end. I want to paint the air which surrounds the bridge, the house, the boat, the beauty of the air in which these objects are located..."
Claude Monet

Artist camps at Edwards Beach, 1890. Mosman Library,

In 1893, the Municipality of the Borough was created, with its council. Mosman became part of a separate municipality. The city of Sydney replaced pedestrian and horse-drawn omnibuses with trams and trains.

The electrical train, introduced from North Sydney to Spit Junction, made it more accessible to travel to the new suburbs and Balmoral Beach. More and more people were eager to buy land and settle in Mosman.

The natural beauty of the bushland, vivid and lush vegetation and proximity to the beach drew the inhabitants of the city and the surroundings. The newfound influx of people to Mosman caused real estate agents to set up business there. The subdivision of the land led to the construction of schools, churches, shops, and services.

Mosman, and its proximity to the city, was a well-frequented ground for visitors before the artist camps were established. Many picnickers came to relax and enjoy the surroundings. The city dwellers were escaping from the stench and the stress of city life. Some even established camps or weekenders. During the depression of the 1890s, they became permanent dwellers. The landowners did not evict them, as they protected their land from the damaging effects of the sand and timber stealers. As time went on, more and more people settled in Mosman. Due to Sydney's housing shortage and to cater for Sydney's housing demands, the subdivision of most of the ridges took place.

Mosman's original inhabitants were the Borogegal and Cammeraygal tribes, living there for 6,000 years or more. They inhabited the bushland, flourishing with angophoras, banksias, grass trees, acacias, and many other plants, which provided them with food. They extracted seeds from the plants for consumption.

Mosman's first artists were members of the Cammeraygal tribe, who painted and carved on the rocks. One can still see the engraving of a fish at Middle Head.

The most renowned Aborigine in Mosman's history was Bungaree. Bungaree was born around 1775 in the traditional aboriginal environment, which his people enjoyed for many thousands of years. However, with the arrival of the Europeans, his life became dramatically different. By the time Bungaree was 20, most of his tribe had died of smallpox. By the time he was 26, he had joined the British explorers on voyages to the far north and had circumnavigated Australia with Matthew Flinders.

Bungaree became the leader of his tribe. He was given land at Georges Head and enjoyed Governor Macquarie's patronage. He lived according to the traditional aboriginal way of hunting and fishing to provide for his family. He welcomed newcomers as their ships entered Sydney Harbour, became friends with the Russian explorers, and was well acquainted with the French. His activities became intriguing reports in the daily newspapers, a well-known Sydney identity. The Europeans' official records, diaries, and published works contained Bungaree's exploits, and descriptions of his lifestyle. His image, painted many times, was exhibited in galleries in London, Paris, and Moscow. Throughout his life, Bungaree gained the respect of his people and the European newcomers to this country. He lived in a cave near the ferry wharf until his death.

However, Bungaree had a talent for mimicking. He was able to imitate how the past governors walked, gestures, and their expressions.

As soon as any ship came through the Sydney Heads, Bungaree would arrive in his fishing boat, rowed by two of his wives. Dressed in an old military jacket, tattered trousers, and his trademark hat, he climbed on board to welcome newcomers to 'his' country. Doffing his hat, bowing deeply, and grinning widely, Bungaree would ask to drink the captain's health in rum or brandy. He then inspected the ship's pantry and levied his 'tribute', which he received in the form of 'presents' or 'loans.'

European history started with Governor Philip at Sydney cove. The flagship of the first fleet, Sirius, on its return from Cape Town in 1789, bringing back food for the starving people in Sydney Cove, became damaged and, in need of repair, sailed to Mosman Bay. As a result, the crew of the first fleet were the first European settlers.

In the late 18th century, artists established camps on Edwards Beach and Little Sirius Cove in Mosman. Part of Mosman Peninsular consisted of Cremorne Point, to the mouth of Long Bay, past the spit in the Middle Harbour, which included small bays and coves linked to the beaches and ridges.

Parts of Sydney had attracted both settlers and pleasure seekers. In 1856, below the Ranges, the western headlands were turned into Cremorne Gardens, emulating the pleasure gardens in London, with fireworks, merry-go-rounds, dancing with band music playing, archery and quoits. Refreshments cost 2 shillings, combined with admission charge and ferry fare from Circular Quay.

Though less striking, other pleasure gardens were opened in Athol Gardens in Shell Cove and in Balmoral, in Hunters Bay and Pearl Bay. The entrepreneur Richard Harnet promoted Mosman Bay as a 'pleasure area.' In 1874, he established regular ferry services, bringing people to see the spectacular waterfalls at the head of the Bay. Dance halls, a weekend hotel, and a quadrille band provided the visitors entertainment.

With its spectacular views of the Middle Harbour, Edwards Beach received its name from a retired soldier who settled there in 1823. He built himself a weatherboard house and lived there on his own. However, much later in the 1880s, young men seeking the pleasure of fresh air, bathing, or swimming, or relaxing on the beach escaped to Edwards Bay.

In the last 25 years of the 19th century, Sydney had the highest standard of living. The exploitation of mineral wealth and the wool industries caused an influx of immigrants to Australia. With the migrants came many artists, who paid a crucial role in the country's cultural development. The artists no longer looked upon the bush as a destructive force. Their works highlighted the beauty, the vibrancy of colours, the charm of the bushland, and the vivid light captured in their paintings.

As the land subdivision continued, Mosman experienced its bursts of development with a significant building boom in 1901. As a result, it became a Federation Suburb, which from the 1920s and 1930s, created a unique style of construction, accomplished by Sydney's most skilled architects. The new residents displayed Mosman's character by drawing artists, writers, intellectuals, and people in business who stoutly maintained the local area's residential nature.

In the late 19th century, Thomas Watling and John Lewis painted members of the Cammeraygal tribe. Conrad Martens (1801–1878), who lived in North Sydney, was the first painter who regularly made sketching trips to Middle Harbour. His sketchbooks revealed the first European records of Mosman Bay and North Head scenes as seen from Balmoral Beach.

> *This a wonderful time when these hours begin,*
> *These long 'small hours of night,*
> *When grass is crisp, and the air is thin,*
> *And the stars come close and bright.*
> *The moon hangs caught in a silvery veil,*
> *From clouds of a steely grey,*
> *And the hard, cold blue of the sky grows pale*
> *In the wonderful Milky Way.*
> *Conrad Martens*

Around the 1880s and 1890s, flocks of artists set camps around Edwards Beach and Little Sirius Cove north of Sydney Harbour. Encouraged by the Impressionist ideals of plein air painting, and the establishment of the Art Society, Mosman became a significant site for the artists.

The first President of the Art Society, John Hoyte, wrote to Sir Henry Parkes:

"There is a great scope in the beautiful scenery surrounding Sydney for those who may confine themselves to landscape painting, and the formation of this society will encourage artists to lend themselves to a faithful representation of that which nature has so bountifully placed within their reach."

Hoyte had worked in the Mosman area, painting the bays of Middle Harbour more than anyone else.

Mosman was a perfect haven for artists, for it provided landscapes on one side and seascapes on the other. Flocks of artists set up camps, imitating France, and parts of the British Isles, following the plein air painting doctrine fostered by the Barbizon and the Impressionist movement. They were free-spirited men, who did not require enormous sums of money to satisfy their creative needs. The dominant idea was to paint outdoors and capture the beauty and the essence of the surroundings. The publication of La Bohème, which promoted anti bourgeoisie way of life, further enhanced Bohemian lifestyle.

Influenced by plein air ideals of painting, many artists established camps at Balmoral Beach and later at the Cove. Other artists joined them, putting up their tents. Far from rough, some constructed wooden floors had carpets, bedsides, and other furniture.

The Bohemian artists were an exciting mix of people in the camps. Many were famous, highly intelligent, literate, wrote poems, and quoted lines from their favourite classical authors. They had minds that questioned societal issues. Often in their leisure time, they had intense arguments with opposing views discussing politics and world affairs. Sometimes the statements were so heady over a few drinks, their voices reverberated throughout the camps. At the end of their heated discussions, they would shake hands and go their merry way. However, in these camps the artists created most of their best paintings.

Livingston Hopkins, who lived in North Sydney, saw Balmoral Beach, and enamoured by its splendour, rented 50 acres of bushland at the beach's northern end. He built a four-room weekender for his pleasure, where he spent most of his weekend's painting and entertaining his Bohemian friends. Hop was a great craftsman. He made a cello, which he often brought with him, and pleasured the guests with his tunes.

Soon after I moved to Sydney, Hop asked me if I had been to Edwards Beach.

"No, not yet. But I believe it is a beautiful beach. People from the city spend their weekends camping there.

"Come and spend next weekend at my camp and I will show you how we live in this paradise.

Of course, it is not what it used to be as most of the campers have disappeared, since the swimmers took over Balmoral and Edwards Beaches, and eventually, my camp became the Bathers Club."

"I was one of the very first to establish my tent at Edwards Beach," said Hop. "When I saw it and its magnificent views across middle Harbour to Sydney heads, I rented 50 acres of land at the northern end of the beach and put up my weekender. I spend most of my time here, painting and entertaining my Bohemian friends. And for a long time, my weatherboard house was the only one at the beach."

"It was no ordinary camp," Hop continued. "I fitted my rooms with orthodox iron bedsteads, a dining tent with a permanent cook installed, who looked after the campers' culinary needs and situated close to a freshwater creek."

Hop took me down to the beach one Sunday, to spend the day there, do some painting and give me a tour of the beach. When I saw the beach, it was indeed a wonder. I watched the distant heads, through which the ships would arrive and then depart, and the camps spread over all this area with the bush in the background. It was an idyllic setting, and an inspiration to paint and lead a carefree existence.

"How does this place get the name Edwards Beach?"

"They named it after a retired soldier who settled here in 1823. He lived here alone in his weatherboard house, but later in the 1880s, other weekend campers joined him. They soon discovered the pleasurable aspects of the beach, the fresh air, the bathing rituals, and freedom from the daily conventions of life.

"During the weekend, sailors from their yacht named Gipsy set up camp at Edwards Beach. They anchored their ship offshore. They created their cricket pitch and were occasionally entertained by a visiting Italian opera company, who arrived in full regalia."

Hop and I spent the day painting and only interrupted it for our lunch break. Old Ben, a retired captain, a master of the field, and a master chef, also described as a 'weather-beaten sea–dog,' full of reminiscences from his past, still lived in a tent in the bush. He served us sausages, and we provided him with beer.

"Let's pack up," said Hop in the late afternoon. "I will take you to the top of the hill to see the view."

We walked through the bush, winding through the antipodean flora, the ground covered with weeds and shrubs. When we reached the top of the hill, I looked at the vista. The evening was gently approaching, and the sky's vibrant pink hue was reflected on the water.

The beauty of the sight from the top of the hill affected my psyche. I decided then, that this piece of land, where I am standing, is where I would build my home.

When we returned to our campsite, we jumped into the water, as it was still light. After a leisurely swim, we sat on the beach, with another pint of beer, while Hop continued to reminisce.

In the evening, Old Ben served us large chunks of cold roast, boiled potatoes, and plum duff, with bread and cake prepared in the camp's oven. Satiated by this feast of culinary delights, we sat outside our tents with our pipes and 'a cheery glass' for a good yarn, reminiscences, music, and laughter.

"One of the most impressive artists I had met several times was Julian Ashton," said Hop. "Have you met him yet?"

"Yes, I have, very briefly at a party. I have heard that he worked on the Picturesque Atlas of Australasia, together with Henry Fullwood, Frank Mahony, and William Macleod. Apparently, it is a very lavish production. They travelled to all parts of Australia and New Guinea. It provided a valuable record of the history of Australia, New Zealand, and the South Pacific during that period."

"It was published in Sydney in 1886 to 1888," continued Hop. "An enormous, multi-volumed Picturesque Atlas of Australia was an attempt, with words and pictures, to describe the Australia of the time. Its publication was one of the most significant cultural projects of the 19th-century Australia."

"I loved his art, and also his ideas," continued Hop. "I invited Julian Ashton to spend a weekend at my artist camp. Julian's attraction to the beach and the way of life brought him regularly to Edwards Beach. He travelled from Bondi, where he lived with his family, and occasionally brought his sons with him. He also loved the open air. There was an old boat, stranded on the sand, and he slept there, even when it was drizzling. Strong, white-haired and ruddy-faced, Ashton had a military-type moustache. All year round, he bathed in the sea. He cultivated his vegetable patch and tended to his poultry.

"Once we were sitting together in the evening, and after a few glasses of wine, he spoke about his father, who was a wealthy American. His mother was the daughter of Count Carlo Rossi, a Sardinian diplomat. His father was an amateur painter and encouraged Julian to pursue his art as a career, recognising his talents. After his father's death, struck by financial difficulties, Julian worked in an engineering firm and later as a draftsman in another. At the same time, he attended art classes in the evening. He left for Paris to study at the new Académie Julian for a few months, and when he returned to London, his works were accepted by the Royal Academy of Arts.

"He became one of the most influential figures in the art world of Sydney. Apart from his works in the Art Gallery of New South Wales as an early Trustee and his significant role in the Art Society of New South Wales, he contributed as a teacher and a painter. Eventually, Julian opened Julian Ashton Art School in Sydney. During the Bohemian artists' generation, he played a significant role and forged the painting style of Australian life and the landscapes.

"Julian, together with Henry Hopwood, established a camp at Balmoral Beach. They painted many Mosman Bay scenes."

"I met Henry Hopwood at the Art Society Exhibition," continued Hop, "where he was exhibiting his paintings. By the time he reached Australia in 1888, he had completed several paintings, while on the ship. One of these paintings, called The Fo Ceas, was exhibited by the Art Society, and purchased by the Art Gallery of New South Wales. Hopwood was a big man with a cheerful demeanour, endowed with a gift for singing and telling yarns. He studied at Académie Julian in Paris. I invited him to become part of my circle. When he returned to England, the Tate Gallery also acquired one of his works created in Australia.

"Benjamin Minns, whom you would know, an Australian-born watercolourist and a Bulletin illustrator, summed up the camaraderie of the camp:

> *'To the t-tree camp, all painters we invite*
> *Including those who work in black and white*
> *Tired workers with a brush or pen*
> *Retreating from the busy haunts of men*
> *Enter our gates and stretch on the grass*
> *Enjoy the soothing pipes and the cooling glass.*
> *Camped on this lonely sea-girt shore*
> *Art is the mistress we adore.'*

"Charles Condor was another patron of the camps. An English-born artist, he arrived in Sydney at 15 and worked in rural NSW as a surveyor's assistant. Condor later shared Minns City Studio and worked with him as an apprentice in the illustrated Sydney News. Julian Ashton recognised Condor's exceptional talent when he was studying under him. He received the Art Society prize for the best painting from nature. The Art Gallery of New South Wales purchased Condor's image, called Little Jetty, painted in 1888."

It was interesting to find out about many artists such as Frank Mahony, William Lister, John Mather, Henry Hopwood, and others who painted here.

"Arturo Steffani was another interesting character who painted in Mosman Bay and was also part of my Bohemian circle of friends. Both a talented artist and an opera singer in Italy, he came to Australia with Lazar's Italian Opera Troupe. After three years, he left the troupe, joined the camp's artists, and contributed richly with his singing and entertainment."

Hop continued with his narrative:

"Women artists could not live in the campsites dictated by the times' customs, but they frequently visited and became enthusiastic artists. The same principle applied to the artists' wives, families, and female guests. They could visit the camps during weekends. Some men even met their wives there.

"Apart from artists, many visitors came to the camps. The famous Robert Louis Stevenson, who spent a night there, presented Old Ben his novel, 'Treasure Island.'

"Impressed by the camp, Ada Cambridge used the centre as a scene in her serial, which she later included in her book 'A Marked Man' in 1891. Ada described the campsite as 'a cluster of tents, a little garden, a Woodstock, water-tub–almost hidden in the trees and bushes until one was close upon it.' The camp looked out towards the great gateway of the heads, seeing ships that passed through and back again."

Other visitors to the camps were writers and illustrators and the editor Archibald who worked for the Bulletin. They all played quoits with Hopkin on the beach. The Bohemians from the Sydney Theatre Co. and music circles were all part of Hop's musical evenings.

The following week, Hop invited Norman Lindsay and Henry to his home, and a great friendship developed between the three of them. They had much in common. What impressed them most was Hop's skilled craftmanship. He made cellos, but he played the instrument and was an accomplished performer. He was exuberant.

Henry Weston, Balmoral & HMAS 'Penguin' on Hill. Private collection

Weston, H. Balmoral Beach. Private Collection. Date unknown

144

Long Sydney, 1905, Clifton Gardens. Mosman Art Gallery, donated by Neil Balnaves AO

Delprat, Paul 1960 a view of Edwards Beach, Balmoral and Middle head from above Burran Ave

Portrait of Bungaree, with Fort Macquarie, Sydney Harbour, in background 1826

15

Curlew Camp

Curlew Camp, before 1890,at Sirius Cove

In 1888, Reuben Brasch established a camp, known as Curlew Camp, close to Mosman Bay. A clothing manufacturer, son of Wolfe Brasch, Reuben was born in Prussia and became prosperous in Melbourne after the Gold Rush. Reuben and his family moved to Sydney from Melbourne and established a department shop in Oxford Street. They lived in an Italianate mansion at Bondi. On weekends, they crossed the harbour from Parsley Bay, and rowed across Little Sirius Cove to their camp.

Curlew Camp was no ordinary camping area. Rueben had engaged a cook called Old Jules, and a young general handyman called Luigi, who had jumped ship some time ago. He catered to the needs of campers who had established a permanent camp; he also helped the artists to carry their easels and canvases across the cove. He had a dog, Esposito, who performed the task of jumping in the water to test the sharks' presence before campers went for a swim. Apart from home comforts, it had a billiard table, a dining tent, a dancing floor, and a small piano.

Curlew Camp was situated in between the trees on the eastern side of the sleepy cove. It had a freshwater creek nearby and a sandy beach around the point. Canvas tents were built around a stone wall that probably contained a bush oven; there were fences to keep the creepers out and wooden walkways to keep feet dry. Simultaneously, a variety of chairs and benches provided a touch of urbanity to its idyllic setting, as they watched ships entering the harbour and making their way into Circular Quay.

Arthur Streeton and Tom Roberts also spent time at the camp. Both left Melbourne for Sydney to extend their sales opportunities. Streeton came first, and Roberts joined him later. While at the campsite, they travelled to other parts of the area to paint landscapes. At the Curlew Camp, both artists created some of their famous works.

While staying at the camps, they taught art classes in the city to earn a living. Roberts taught portrait painting in studios in the town and became one of Sydney's most famous painters for portraits.

The depression at the time was going through its worst phase. Life was difficult for the artists. Waiting for the news of the sale of their paintings, they spent time at Growler's Corner in the Cafe Francis. At that time, the only work available from time to time were portrait commissions from the Bulletin.

Even though Tom Roberts lived in a tent, whenever he visited the city to search for portrait commissions, he made a point of dressing elegantly, which impressed his fellow artists.

Souter, described Tom Roberts as:

"Our sole society Bohemian, Tom Roberts wore his crushed hat and red cape with more dignity than many a king wearing his coronation robe and crown. He represented a successful artist with an entry to the government house and was on the dining list of people who had a couple of thousand a year."

Tom Roberts was a man of two worlds. His love for England never left him, but Australia was close to his heart, and he loved the uniqueness of the Australian bush and landscapes. Tom painted shearers, drovers, and bushrangers. He was an original thinker, a prolific reader with vast knowledge, will, and a determination to succeed. A gifted raconteur, he was always the life of the party, and enjoyed the friendship of others. Roberts loved music, especially music by Beethoven, Schubert, and Wagner. He was ready to give his time to those who needed it. He had a strong British accent and spoke in a bright, penetrating tone.

Women came for pleasure and entertainment, but they could not stay overnight. Camps were hidden in the bush, in a private sanctuary, away from the rest of the world. A painting by Streeton was of the view of Sydney Harbour with naked women, 'nymphs', cavorting on their way down to the camp. It was a time of merriment and playfulness, with wine and beer flowing.

Apart from Streeton and Roberts, another well-known artist who painted at the Curlew Camp was Henry Fullwood, who joined the artists at Curlew Camp when he lost all his savings in the 1883 bank crash. Henry Fullwood was named 'Remus', as he was a talented storyteller. He remained there until he married in 1895.

Daplyn was a frequent visitor, and Hinton, who lived in a camp at Balmoral Beach, was also a regular visitor to Curlew Camp; he had bought many camp paintings for his collection, which became part of the New England Gallery.

William Marshall-Hall, a London based composer and teacher, often visited the camps and enjoyed the Bohemian camaraderie. He later became the first professor of music at Melbourne University.

Julian Ashton, who occasionally visited the campsite, recalled:

"I saw Streeton fairly often. He lived in a camp at Little Sirius Cove, Mosman, where Tom Roberts joined him later. He used to do the marketing, and, on arriving at the Musgrave Street wharf, had to walk around the point and blow a whistle for the boat to come across from the camp. To see him returning on Saturday nights, laden with parcels of bread, beer, and beef, and as merry as a boy at a picnic was a delight. In those days, the painters' material wants were few, but their hopes were unbounded."

Streeton, who loved quoting Keats in 1890, while still at the camp, wrote a florid description of the surroundings and his life in the camps.

"I sit here in my tent and look across the little bay beneath to the hill beyond, all in massive purple shadow–right across which comes a beautiful mass of clematis and begonia creeper, the stem of a red gum sapling and a young wild cherry tree. Below a few feet, is my box, with mignonette opening its second set of leaves to the sun's brilliant warmth, which floods all the green and cheerful surroundings of our tent, making it like a fairy's bower. All the morning, I've been wondering about the hill of bush behind our camp gathering flowers and delicate ferns to plant in our little summer house close by."

In 1896, he wrote:
"Australia was a young country. It had no culture, no castles, no abbeys, no folk songs. There was no Bloomsbury, or Montmartre, or Latin Quarter of Paris with its exciting Bohemian life—no one was interested in art or literature. It was crude, materialistic, and Philistine."

Norman Lindsay expressed that "Australians were nonchalant about art and generally showed very little interest. The young were encouraged to travel to Europe to experience the environment, which was abundant in the cultural sense and recognised their artistic career."

The first artist to travel to Europe was Adelaide Ironside, who went to England. She eventually settled in Rome and gained international recognition. One by one, there was an exodus of artists. Condor left for good, and Streeton and Roberts became war artists. John Peter Russel went to Paris and studied in the same school as Toulouse Lautrec, Van Gogh, and Emile Bernard. Russel worked in the south of France and became friendly with Monet and Matisse. He had introduced colour painting to young Matisse, who was impressed by his colour art. Russel's work was more known in France than in Australia.

George Washington Lambert was an animated character and colourful figure, named 'Ginger' because of his curly moustache and red hair. He had worked in the Bulletin as an illustrator and won a travelling scholarship. Lambert worked as a portrait artist and received a commission in Europe. Returning to Australia, he received a state welcome.

Even though these artists lived overseas most of the time, other exceptional artists who became famous and contributed to Australian art were Rupert Bunny, Emanuel Philip Fox, John Longstaff, and Hugh Ramsay. Rupert Bunny and Fox both studied at the Melbourne School of Art. Fox's primary interest was in portraiture painting. Bunny favoured painting women in an Edwardian style, sitting outside on the balconies, and drinking tea, at leisure.

As a portrait painter, he received many commissions from the Prince and Princess of Wales, Queen Alexandra, many counts and countesses, Australian prime ministers, and many more. Hugh Ramsay, a most talented artist and a gifted musician, studied at the National Gallery School in Victoria. He left for the fashionable Paris Art School Colarossi, where many great European artists received their training.

The experience of studying overseas and the cultural experience had benefitted these artists greatly. With the undeveloped state of Australia's art, they needed to study abroad to gain new skills and confidence. They came back to Australia with new ideas and culturally enriched the Australian art world.

Art schools, galleries, and art societies were dreary and had little to offer in those days. Eager young artists and art students were attracted to the camps—at Box Hill, at Eaglemont and in the Yarra Valley, and at Sirius Cove on Sydney Harbour—drifting in and out.

"All, scattered in the afterlife around the world, recalled nostalgically the zest for life and the work that filled the days and nights of the camps of the 1890s."

With the legalising of daylight bathing, the Bohemian style of the camp dwellers came to an end around 1903.

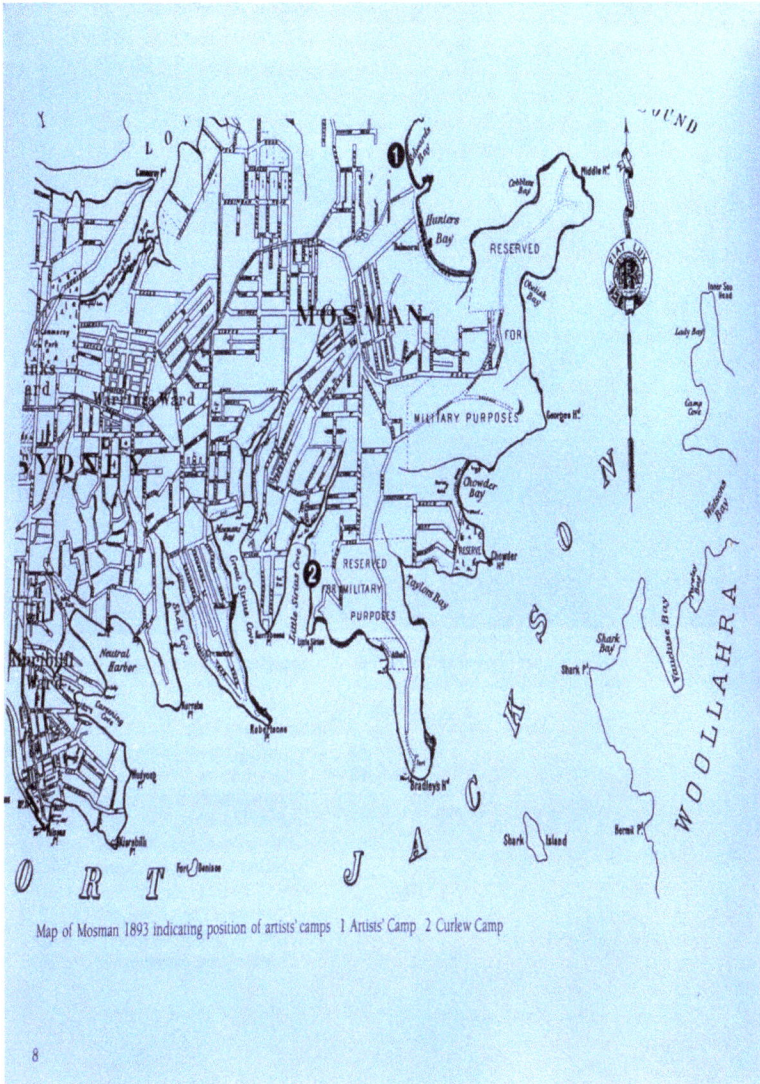

Map of Mosman 1893 indicating position of artists' camps 1 Artists' Camp 2 Curlew Camp

Map of Mosman 1893, including position of artists' camps. 1. Artists' Camp, 2 Curlew Camp

Streeton Arthur, Sirius Cove, 1890. Art Gallery of NSW

Roberts, Tom. Cremorne Point,1894, National Gallery of Victoria

Roberts, Tom. Cremorne Point, 1894, National Gallery of Victoria

16

A New Home

While working for the Bulletin, and during his break, Henry was reading the property columns as he usually did, and suddenly his eyes caught sight of an advertisement:

This Mosman property has just become available after the death of its owner in England. A prime piece of land with 17,000 square feet of land, on a hill with spectacular views of the Harbour, the Heads on both sides, enclosing Castle Rock, Clontarf, and Middle Harbour. The buyer has the potential to subdivide and sell.

It was the same site Henry was interested in and waiting for to come on the market. He rang the estate agent right away and went to meet him. It was a large parcel of land, just as advertised.

Henry was also a businessman and calculated the value and possibilities of the land for a future outcome. Without hesitation, he bought the property. As soon as he got home, he rang Ruth and told her the news.

"Ruth, you would love it. It has a magnificent water view, perfect for swimming at the beach, which Lizzie would love. It will become a prestigious area once the streets are established. I will organise for you to come over and view the land. I am sure you will be happy with it. You have a chance to meet and get to know the friends I made who are also my workmates. I am sure you will like Sydney."

"It sounds fantastic, and I do miss you so very much. At least I will get to see you and spend some time with you."

"All right, my dear, I will take a week's holiday, and we will have a wonderful time. I can't wait to show you the property."

When Ruth finished speaking to Henry, she was excited. But when she thought about Charles and leaving him behind, sadness overcame her, torn between her love for her husband and a child that she bore.

After seeing the property and the view from the hilltop, the ocean's incessantly moving sceneries, the white sandy beaches, she was amazed and overwhelmed. It reminded her of Wynyard and the beach where she spent her summer days with family and friends.

"It is beautiful, Henry."

They went down to the beach, walking along the sand.

Ruth noticed artists were sitting at various spots, sketching; others sat with their easels, adding colour to their work. It was a bright sunny day, with only a gentle breeze blowing. A few small boats were sailing on the harbour. They sat on the sand for a little while, gazing at the far horizon and enjoying the silence and each other's company.

"Let's go for a walk in the bush," said Henry.

"Can you imagine, 20 years ago artists lived and painted here in campsites? There was a genuine camaraderie amongst these Bohemian men who led a simple life with very little money. Still, they just wanted to paint the Australian bush and its landscapes, experimenting with a new painting style, which had evolved in France.

"Even the artists who were still very English found something magical in the Australian countryside," Henry continued. "I will take you to Mosman Bay, where the artists had camped. There is a pathway through the bush which will take us there."

On their way, they came across many clusters of angophoras.

"The artists loved painting these angophoras because of their exciting structures, which were visible on the other side of the harbour."

They passed banksias, acacias, and grass trees, and enjoyed nature. The chirping of the birds was audible, and finally, they arrived at Mosman Bay.

"This is where Streeton and Tom Roberts painted. Its original name was Sirius Cove, which was named by Governor Phillips' flagship, HMS Sirius, careened and refitted in the bay in 1789.

"I think I have shown you enough for one day. We need to get back home and have a rest before we have dinner with my workmates and their wives. I think it would be interesting for you to meet some of them. They are looking forward to meeting you."

Two days after Ruth left, Henry got word that the council had passed the building plans. He rang Ruth first, and then rang the builders, informing them of the good news, and commenced organising his home's construction.

Henry started designing the house even before the settlement of the purchase. His idea was to build an English farmhouse-style mansion with red brick walls, using western red cedar-shingles on the pitched roof angled at 45 degrees. He also wanted to render some brick walls and paint them white.

In the early 1890s, another novel feature was an Australian discovery, using double cavity and double glazing to provide insulation. The veranda was another feature introduced to suit the Australian climate. Henry created a large patio, using exposed ironbark timber with beams and Romanesque style columns. It would be suitable for the Australian environment, but it would become an outdoor area where he could entertain his artist and literary friends. Gregarious by nature, Henry was a member of many clubs and organisations and enjoyed the camaraderie and entertaining—he was a 'bon vivant.'

Since there were no roads to get to the house, the building material had to be shipped across by boat to the construction site. They would have to be offloaded and carried up the ridge to the higher grounds. Henry found a well-known building company for the construction of the house. It had an excellent reputation and was also well-known to him.

Towards the end of the Federation era, the builders started the construction of the house. It was large, more like a mansion with exciting features, but not as ornate as a Federation home. On either side of his house were two large blocks of land, which, if he wished, he could sell them sometime in the future.

Henry was very much involved with the construction of his dream home. One of the most exciting features of the house was a high gabled roof. It had very detailed fretwork. The house had lynched gates and picket fences.

Builders constructing such houses would usually place two carpenters on the property. According to Henry's design, these tradesmen would set out the shape of the house. Next came the excavation of the footings, and supervision of the bricklaying as the walls go up. Once they reach the bottom level, they made the windows onsite, measure to the required size, hand-cut the roofing frames and gables, and constructed the same when ready.

All materials came by barge, sourced from local suppliers. There was no electricity until around the 1930s. Gas was the primary source of power, and all houses had a name. Henry called his home 'The Beacon'; as the ships entered the Sydney Harbour, they would use his house as a guide. It took 12 months to finish, and then was ready to move into.

17

Christmas

The songbirds were beginning to sing, rejoicing, and announcing the coming of the festive season. I was looking forward to spending Christmas Eve with my family in Hobart and bringing them to our new home in Sydney.

I thought about my life as a child, and our Christmas family celebrations. Unlike in Australia, where Christmas day was more significant, my parents celebrated Christmas Eve and continued with the customs of their forefathers.

My father decorated the Christmas tree on the morning of Christmas Eve with colourful decorations from Germany; bells jingled in the breeze, bright baubles, wooden ornaments of angels, Santa Claus and many more. As my father decorated the tree, he sang German Christmas songs. His favourites were 'O Tannenbaum' and 'Stille Nacht, Heilige Nacht.' It must have been the only time in the year that he sang.

After a hearty meal of goose, with boiled potatoes and red cabbage, we would open our Christmas presents. I thought about my only son, with whom I could not share this wonderful time.

It was difficult for my parents to start a new life in a new country, without the language skills to communicate with the others, but luckily, a few German friends were living nearby to support each other. My father was stubborn, and nothing would prevent him from learning the language and being part of society. He was a man who valued education and did well enough to get into a school in Hamburg and finish his four years with high marks.

My father had a love of literature and philosophy. He spent his free time reading books, primarily from the Baroque period. The time of enlightenment produced fascinating modern literature with Herder, Goethe, and Friedrich Schiller. His grandfather Wilhelm passed on his love of reading to his son and grandson. From when I was a young child, I could still remember how my father read me stories from Fairy Tales, which he later gave me to keep. Often, I would pick it up and admire the old German calligraphy with beautifully hand-drawn pictures.

Early childhood memories flooded my mind: memories of Collinsvale, the people, the friends I had, freedom to wander around in the bush, the creek that I loved to sit by the bank and let my imagination fly.

Lizzie, dressed up in a red Christmas dress with a red ribbon on her hair, was excitedly waiting to see her father. Henry's parents were also there to celebrate and were eager to see their son. As soon as the doorbell rang, Lizzie raced to the door, opened it, and gave her father a big hug. After greeting Ruth, he wished his parents

"Frohe Weihnachten," and kissed them and the rest of the family, wishing them a happy Christmas. They all sat down for a drink and some nibbles. Lizzie went over and sat with her father.

"Ruth," her mother said, "you leave everything to me. I will organise the meal. You go and talk to Henry."

She went and sat with Henry.

"Hello, my darling girl," said Henry with a kiss.

"Oh Henry, I am so glad to see you again, and I hope we will never be apart from each other for so long."

"I'm so glad to see you, papa. I hope you never go away again," said Lizzie, hugging him.

Soon dinner was ready, and the family moved to the table. Red candles flooded the wooden table. In the middle stood a tall vase with red holly berry pinecones. The dinner was turkey with vegetables, baked potatoes, cranberry sauce, and a Christmas pudding for dessert.

It was time for giving gifts. Ruth had bought some riding boots for Lizzie.

"I love them," said Lizzie. "Can we go riding tomorrow, daddy?"

"Yes, I will take you tomorrow afternoon." Then came another present from Henry, a wind jacket. Lizzie was ecstatic.

"I can wear the jacket as well...."

The following morning, Ruth and Henry went to visit Charles. Ruth took gifts for him, and his favourite chocolates. As soon as he saw his mother, he started shaking and moving in his bed with excitement. Charles wasn't sure about Henry, who went over and kissed him.

As soon as he opened his present and saw the car and the book, he wanted Ruth to read it to him straight away.

Henry went for a walk while Ruth read to Charlie. Charlie looked intensely at the pictures in the book. Was he trying to work out what was going on in the story? He suddenly looked tired and closed his eyes. She closed the book, took his hand, looked at him tearfully, and was overcome with grief. Henry walked in and saw her distraught state. He gently freed her hand from Charlie's, took her in his arms, and comforted her. Just then, the nurse came in. It was time to leave. Ruth said goodbye to Charlie while he was asleep, unable to stop the tears in her eyes as she stroked and kissed him. It would be the last time she would see him for a while.

The following day, Henry took Lizzie riding and spent half a day with her. In the afternoon, he went to visit his parents. Ruth had often called on them, and they were happy to see her and catch up with Henry's news.

On the last evening, before they left, the family had gathered in the lounge room, chatting. Ruth had spoken to her mother about selling the farm and buying Ruth and Henry's house.

"At least you will be closer to the girls and be able to keep an eye on Charles," said Ruth.

"I had been thinking about just that." When Henry brought up the subject again, Mrs Callaway agreed to it. The girls were happy, as both were in Hobart. They would be able to stay with their mother.

Two days later, the Weston family boarded the ship for Sydney.

18

Move to Sydney

It was a long trip from Hobart to Sydney. For Lizzie, it was a novel and exciting experience. She went for a walk to explore the ship. From time to time, Ruth digressed from the scenery in front and around her to thoughts of Charles.

"How is he going to feel not seeing me? Will he miss me or forget me? Will the nurses treat him well? At least my family will be able to visit him. For that, I am so grateful."

"A penny for your thoughts," said Henry, taking her in his arms and looking at her warmly.

"I was thinking about Charlie; how will he be when I am not there?"

"Oh! He will be fine. Besides, you will visit him from time to time. You can spend the school holidays with him. Lizzie would love to see her grandma again. You know how much she loves her."

"You are right," said Ruth. But she still felt a pang of guilt within her for leaving him behind. She turned and looked at him. "I am so happy to be with you, Henry, after such a long separation."

"So am I. You know how much I love you and all the sacrifices you have made for me." He leaned over and kissed her gently on her lips.

They sat silently and watched the ocean. The waves started moving backwards and forwards with a significant force. From time to time, the motion of the ship was getting stronger. Ruth felt squeamish. She got up. "I think I will go inside and lie down a bit." Just as she left, Lizzie came out.

"This is getting scary," she said, looking at the waves. Suddenly the storm started, and they both ran inside to take shelter. Fortunately, it was all over in two hours, and the clouds cleared up.

After a long journey on the ship, the Westons arrived safely in Sydney. When they saw the house, both Lizzie and Ruth were amazed. They had an idea what the house would look like from Henry's description and photographs, but they were surprised to see the place and the house looking so grand. They turned away from their home and looked around.

"There are no houses near us. Are we the only ones living here?" Lizzie called out.

"There is a house on the left, but it is not visible from here because of the trees and the bush surrounding it."

"And no roads," Ruth remarked.

"Unfortunately, it has been problematic because of the winding, steep, divided roads, and dead ends. Eventually, they will build the streets. There are cleared tracks to Mosman proper."

"Let's look at the inside," Lizzie said excitedly. She rushed in.

"Oooh!" she exclaimed. "This is huge, and the ceiling is so high. Where is my bedroom, papa?"

"Upstairs, on the right. Would you like to have a look?"

She ran up the stairs, and when she saw her room, she was not disappointed. The windows were facing east with the view of the harbour. "Wow," she exclaimed and ran downstairs again to join the family.

"I love my room," said Lizzie. "It is much larger than my room in Hobart, and I have a view of the harbour."

They took their time to investigate their new home and were pleased that their furniture had already arrived. Ruth and Lizzie went to unpack, while Henry started arranging the table with the help of one of his colleagues, who came by ferry to give him a hand and brought some food.

The following day, Henry took Lizzie and Ruth to Mosman town to acquaint them with the shops. They hired a horse and buggy to transport them to the village. In Mosman proper, and in the vicinity, trams and horse and buggy were the modem of transport from town to some outskirts. They were also used for household garbage collections, transporting building materials, household deliveries such as milk, bottles of water, bread and ice and night soil; and even the fire brigades used them.

The Westons dismounted at the corner of Military Road and Raglan Street.

"Military Road," explained Henry, "gets its name because the road was developed to bring artillery to the defence sites along Middle Head Road, Bradley's Head, and George's Heights. This was done to protect the city against any enemy attacks as they entered the harbour."

Ruth noticed the greengrocers right at the corner.

"Oh!" she exclaimed. "I must go in and talk to the greengrocer about the deliveries."

She went and introduced herself.

"I am Ruth Weston. We have just moved to Mosman, and I was wondering when you deliver fruit and vegetables."

"Call me Joe, Mrs Weston. I deliver on Thursday mornings. Let me know what you need and the delivery information, and I will do that, no problem."

She bought some fruit and vegetables before she left.

"Thank you, Joe. I will phone you in the next couple of days and place my order."

"On the left," said Henry, "is the Buena Vista Hotel and the wine shop called the Plonk Bar."

"Dad, you will be able to get all your wines from there," said Lizzie.

"Not a bad idea," said Henry with a smile.

They noticed the bakery on the opposite side, and further on, as they walked past Avenue Road, the butcher and the chemist were there.

"There is the Mosman School, where you will be going," remarked Ruth. Lizzie looked at her in silence.

"Come on, Lizzie. You will have a great time there," said, Henry. Just then, Lizzie saw the picture theatre.

"Oh!" she exclaimed. "Can we go to the movies one day, please, please? I have never been to see a movie."

170

The picture theatre was called the Kinema Picture Show, known as the 'Flicks.' Young men, dressed in white coats and caps, would come into the theatre, and serve ice creams, mints, chocolates, lollies, and peanuts, carrying trays on their shoulders. Then Lizzie spied a milk bar next door to the cinema.

"I would like some ice cream, please," said Lizzie.

They all thought it was a good idea. They stopped at the bakery to get some freshly made bread. They bought bread, meat pies, and cream puffs for lunch. When they had finished their tour of Mosman town and their shopping, they got into their horse-drawn buggy and returned home.

Part Five

19

Henry's Venture

After moving to Sydney, I decided to open my own advertising company. I had mentioned to Hop that I was keen to start my business.

"Henry, you are not just a talented artist, but you also have a good business acumen. As you know, I will retire soon, and you will be able to get projects from the Bulletin."

"Mosman, as you know, is growing by leaps and bounds. People are building homes, especially around me, and they are looking for architects to design their homes. I would love to be involved in designing houses, and at the same time, continue with creating cartoons, illustrating, and painting."

I found a shop right in the centre of the city's business sector, which I converted into a studio agency called The Weston Company. In the 1920s, the artists created advertisements in black and white, using the new emerging art forms. My first publication was designing the cover for the Society of the Black and White Artists. I produced artworks and sold advertising, and slowly, I started getting work. My first three black-and-white creations were for advertising tobacco.

Weston H, Cover design for the Lone Hand, 1914 (Caban GP page 61)

My NSW and Queensland Railway Department advertisement for 'Halcyon Holidays in North Queensland' appeared in Lone Hand on November 1, 1909.

Soon, word got around, and I received contracts from multiple clients to design posters. One of them was for Dunlop Rubber.

I also published a book of caricatures,

All's Well with the Fleet,' with 12 brilliantly coloured lithographs featuring sailors in various forms of trouble. I continued to contribute cartoons and caricatures to the Bulletin. I also illustrated Australian books, published by NSW Bookstall, covering stories and illustrations for Lone Hand and Steele Rudd's Dad in Politics, as well as postcards, poems, and verses.

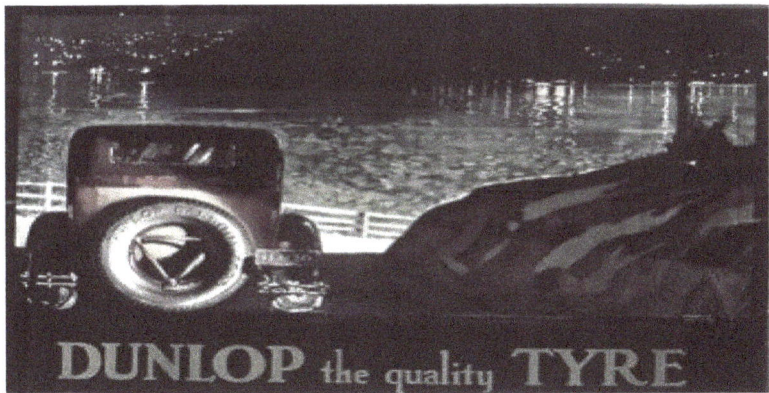

Weston H, Advertisements illustrated for various clients.

Cover design by Harry Weston 1904

A TRAGEDY,

The Girl: "What was th' worse
thing'appened to yer on yer last voyage, Bill?
'Bill: "Well, we struck a rock,
lost our rudder, th' cap'n
died o'cholera,
th'first mate was lost overboard;
but worst of all, I ran out of
VICE-REGAL SMOKING MIXTURE!

Cover designed by Harry Weston, 1904, for W.D and H.O. Wills

Old Lady: "Don't cry, little boy! Are you hurt?"/ Little Boy: "No, but I will be. I dropped father's CAPSTAN TOBACCO down the drain.

Sydney Art Society's art exhibition was coming up. I had been preparing a collection of paintings of the Mosman bush and the Balmoral seascape. Australian nature always had a certain mystical quality to me, and in my images, I wanted to express the spirit of the land. I painted my landscapes at dusk. The moon's reflection on the water created romantic hazes of pink, mauve, and orange. My paintings sold well. I made quite a few small landscape paintings, and those with a limited budget bought them. In 1907, I was part of the Australian Society of Artists' Club in Sydney's' selection committee, which I enjoyed immensely.

In 1924, the Black and White Artists' Club opened in the city, which I joined. The members met in pubs or studios of cartoonists based in the town, as they worked for Smith's Weekly and the Daily Guardian, which were close to them. On Saturdays, they frequented the pubs, with money in their hands after being paid on Friday. The Black and White Society of Australia was the first in the world.

Australian Society of Artists, selection committee, 1907, indoor picnic after selecting works. Harry Weston is third from the left. Josef Lebovic Gallery. Mosman Art Gallery coll.

The end of the 19th century saw many changes that transformed Western society: the effects of industrialisation, the invention of cars, and the popularity of photography. In late 19th-century Britain, a new art form was coming into vogue known as Art Nouveau. From there, it spread to Europe, America, and Australia. Art Nouveau evolved from Impressionism, but went in a different direction, away from the boundaries of its historical evolution. It incorporated arts and crafts, furnishings, and symbolic and applied arts.

Inspired by organic and geometric shapes, the artists created elegant, flowing lines with muted tones. They emphasised contours and took inspiration from Japanese art and exotic oriental forms, especially Japanese prints' floral and curved patterns. The artists painted idealised women—feminine, slender, attractive, with long flowing hair—as sexual beings, and often they painted them naked. It was a period when women were working, independent, and had more freedom.

Art Nouveau in Australia was popular in many arts and craft forms, such as Australian Flora and Fauna as decorative art in fabrics. Colour was also a fundamental principle in this new art form. The use of colours such as mauves, ochres, pinks, and soft greens, instead of the natural colours of the bush. Architecture, interior design, glass, and posters used decorative art.

Sydney Long was the first Australian to experiment with the Art Nouveau style in his Australian landscape paintings. Long had taken the bush and gave it a mysterious and romantic quality. His mythical characters, gipsies, and pans frolicked harmoniously in the bush setting. The Art Gallery of NSW bought his painting called Fantasy.

However, Art Nouveau declined just before WWI and made way for a new form of art, Art Deco. The effect of the industrial revolution on Art Deco, with its impact on machine-made objects, made the designs more symmetrical and streamlined.

Art Nouveau designs by Liberty and Company, using interlaced floral motifs, became very popular in England Art Nouveau and Art Deco designs were used for furniture coverings, curtains, and cushions

I designed Art Nouveau houses for my clients, using some of the technical innovations of the late 19th century, such as exposed iron, oversized and irregular shapes of glasses. Art Nouveau paintings and soft furnishing fabrics appealed to them. I created paintings on their walls and found decorators to furnish their homes using Art Deco fabrics.

I experimented with Art Nouveau English poster designs in some of my works, with flowing lines, flat tones, and silhouettes. For me, art was something natural and organic. The beauty of nature exists in its raw form, colour, and shape. Art Nouveau was not popular in Australia, and by the mid-20s, it vanished, followed by Modernism and post Modernism.

Grace Cossington Smith, 1915, *Quaker girl*, AGV

Ruth Sutherland, 1910, *Girl in a hammock*, AGV

Karl Schmidt-Rottluff, Dr Rosa Schapire,1919

Wassily Kandinsky, no.7 from the *Kleine Welten* (Small worlds) series, published 1922

20

Ruth's Work

After Ruth and Lizzie returned from Hobart, Ruth started focusing on her life in Sydney. With the work in the garden completed, she got heavily involved in social activities. Her priority was to join an organisation, and she found the Sydney City Mission, where she worked two days a week. She also became involved with the women's refuge centre and worked there one day a week. Ruth saw women suffering from hunger, with bruises, beaten by their husbands, who came twice a week for food and clothing.

Ruth decided to hold functions at her home to raise money for the orphanage. She invited wives of politicians, artists, and mothers from Mosman Primary, whom she befriended. Often, Ruth asked musical groups, who gave up their time freely, to entertain the women. She organised speakers involved with organisations to speak and inform the women about such organisations and what the government was doing to assist them. Through these meetings, often, a few women would also join in to help.

Christmas was approaching, and festivities had started.

Ruth decided a month before Christmas to hold a function at her home, this time to raise money for the Women's Refuge Centre. She had invited 60 guests. Ruth had helpers from the women involved in the centre who assisted her with the cooking. It was a smorgasbord affair, and each couple had to pay for the meal and bring a bottle of wine. However, beer was part of the meal.

The guests arrived, including some from Burran Ave. Most of the guests were dressed in Christmas attire to celebrate the upcoming festive season and support the cause of helping the needy. There was a large jar, written 'Donations Accepted', with a caricature of a man sitting behind it on the table in the foyer, dressed as Santa Claus and peeping from the side, smiling. Henry stood near the large ceramic jar and let no one go past without placing a coin inside it.

Dr Charles just made his way and stood in front of the jar.

"What's all this nonsense? I have paid for my meal already, and now I must pay again?"

"Just drop in a coin or two, mate, then you can join the crowd on the balcony," said Henry jovially.

"And what if I don't have a coin?"

"Notes are welcome."

"Well, I better drop in a coin then. Otherwise, I can't go past you."

Dr Charles noticed his chess friend, Joe mingling with the crowd, and went over and joined him.

Some guests were standing on the veranda, watching the beautiful sunset, radiant and opalescent in bright red and yellow, casting its hues on the glistening water. The distant land with trees and shrubs were ghostly shadows.

After an hour and a half of intermingling, and greeting old and new friends, dinner was announced. Tables of six or eight were arranged on the large, covered veranda and some inside. Handmade embroidered white linen tablecloths adorned the tables; each had a posy made from flowers picked from the garden.

The guests were served a sumptuous meal of roast turkey, pork with roast potatoes, and various vegetables.

"Delicious food," remarked Dr Charles, returning to the table with a plate full of food.

"A man seldom thinks with more earnestness of anything, than he does of his dinner."

"That was by Samuel Johnson, who loved his food."

Dr Charles continued entertaining the guests at his table with jokes and tales:

"There was a man whose last name was Rose. As a lark, he named his daughter Wild, with the happy conceit of having her called Wild Rose. But that sentiment was 'knocked out' when the woman grew up to marry a man whose last name was Bull."

Just then, Henry got up to give a speech regarding the fundraising for the orphanage and thanked the ladies involved for their superb meal and Ruth for organising it.

"These volunteers are doing splendid work. Well, it's time now for dessert, so I am told."

The desserts looked superb: the traditional Christmas pudding, bread and butter pudding, fruit trifle. Fruit salad and ice cream.

"There is only one difference between a long life and a wonderful dinner," said Dr Charles, quoting Robert Louis Stevenson, "At dinner, the sweets come last."

21

Lizzie's Discovery

Lizzie soon settled into her new life in Mosman. At first, starting in a new school was a dilemma that she had to face. Her nervousness took over, not knowing anyone and wondering whether she would find a friend. Her teacher, Mrs Woodward, whom the students called 'Woody,' put her at ease. Soon she settled in and made some friends.

She loved swimming, and she spent most weekends with her friends at Balmoral Beach, swimming, and sunbathing. She was in the swimming team for her age group and won her races easily. Lizzie also found a friend who was not so dissimilar to her. Helen was also a bright child, but not an excellent student. Both spent a lot of time together—however, little time on schoolwork.

On the weekends, Henry would take Lizzie to Balmoral Beach for fishing. Fish were abundant in the water. Sometimes they went to the rocks, found oysters, winkles, and pipis, took the catch home, cooked them, and ate them with home-grown potatoes.

Before long, Ruth had established a garden with herbs and vegetables, tomatoes, potatoes, and lemon trees;

and planted a myriad of flowering plants, such as birds of paradise, azaleas, and arum lilies. Once a week came a supply of food and a postman on a horse delivering parcels and letters.

Ferries would bring picnickers from Circular Quay in the summer making a round trip from Nielson Park, Clifton Gardens, and Balmoral Wharf. Visitors would be going to the beach, parkland, and the vacant blocks along the Esplanade. Much entertainment took place at the beach, such as pony rides, the miniature steam railway, roundabouts, and chair-o-planes; and, not to mention, food delights such as ice cream for the children, lolly shops, doughnuts, and fairy floss. In the 1920s during the summer, Dance Halls lit up along the Esplanade would open, playing music from the 20s.

Every Sunday morning, Sunday School Mission would arrive. First, they would put up the enormous banner, and the man with the portable organ would be setting up. At the Peggy's Rocks, at the bottom of Raglan Street, the local children, visitors, and adults would arrive, listen to the service, and sing songs, followed by Bible stories.

Ruth had settled in at her new home. She was kept busy as she started volunteering at Sydney City Mission, which provided the needy with food, clothing, and even houses. Ruth worked there two days a week. She had made friends through Henry's engagement with the art societies, clubs, and work. She did excursions with them, and frequently entertained them at her home.

Henry loved to party at the drop of a hat. Often, he invited interstate guests to spend a weekend with them. From time to time, Henry's parents came for a visit. Ruth was fond of them, and she enjoyed their company. With the completion of the construction of the new roads in Mosman, Ruth now had two more neighbours near her, with whom, so far, she had no contact.

One day, Lizzie woke up, and pretended to have a headache and body aches.

"You can stay home and recover," said her mother. "But I need to go out as it is my day at the Sydney City Mission."

"I will be fine," said Lizzie. "I will just stay in bed."

As soon as Ruth left, Lizzie jumped out of her bed, showered and prepared her breakfast. She sat outside and watched the view of the beach. It was a perfect summer morning; the sun was slowly raising its head. She sat there for an hour, daydreaming. She got up, went inside, got her book and read for another hour.

Then suddenly, she decided to go for a walk down to the beach. As no one was around, only a few distant boats, she took her dress off, and went for a swim. When she finished, she rushed home, changed her underwear, washed her wet clothes, and hung them outside to dry before her mother returned.

She then decided to explore her parents' bedroom. Lizzie looked around. "It is not dissimilar to the room in Tasmania," she thought, "only they have arranged the furniture differently to take full advantage of the view of the water." She opened their clothing cupboard to see how they had organised their clothes. Both had different hanging spaces. She then went through the chest of drawers. There were knick-knacks, jewellery, and letters that her mother had always saved. Opening the second shelf, she found some photos that Ruth had not yet put in the photo album. She then opened the bottom drawer, which contained private papers, such as the house sale in Hobart, their present property information, birth certificates. She took out her birth certificate and behind it was an added page about her adoption, that her mother had died at childbirth. There was no information regarding her birth father.

Lizzie stayed rooted to the ground, in shock. "Am I adopted? Why didn't they tell me I was not theirs? No wonder I don't look like any of them." She read the information about her adoption repeatedly. She closed the drawer shut, went into her bedroom, and began sobbing.

Lizzie heard her mother coming.

Ruth put her things down on the table and went straight into Lizzie's room to see how she was.

"What is the matter, Lizzie? Have you been crying? Are you all right?" She burst into tears again. Ruth came over, sat on her bed, and tried to touch her.

"Don't touch me," she said in anger. "I am not your daughter. I found my birth certificate. Why have you been hiding it from me?"

Somewhat shocked, Ruth went over and sat next to Lizzie.

"Listen, Lizzie, we wanted to tell you, but we decided to wait till you were old enough to understand fully. We thought once you had settled in our new home, we would tell you. You found out by going through our papers, which you should not have done."

"We adopted you because we could not have any children. I desperately wanted to have a child but unfortunately couldn't." Then Ruth explained to her how she came into her life and how happy it made them because they had a daughter now.

"From the very first day we brought you home, we loved you and cared for you as parents do."

"Does Grandma know about me?"

"Yes, she does, and so do your aunts. Grandma came with me to help me and advise me, and then she stayed with me for weeks to take care of you. You were not a straightforward child, you know. You cried a lot."

Lizzie remained in her room. She thought about her birth parents; she wondered how they looked. Why did her mother commit suicide? There was no information about her father. Where could he be? She suddenly got up to find her mother. Ruth was sitting outside, deep in thought and drinking her tea. Lizzie came quietly and sat down.

"Lizzie, would you like some lunch, dear?" she asked gently.

"No, thanks, I am not hungry. I was wondering if you had a photo of my mother." Ruth's heart missed a beat. "But I am her mother," she thought.

"I don't, Lizzie, but I could get one for you. She was a pretty girl."

"No, it doesn't matter." She got up and left.

When Henry came home, he found her outside wandering around in the garden. When she saw him, she came over and sat down.

"I need to tell you something. Lizzie knows she is adopted."

"Did you tell her?"

"No, I didn't. Lizzie surreptitiously went into our bedroom, looked through the drawers, and found out. We should have told her earlier. Now she is very distraught and is in her room and hasn't been out all afternoon, except to ask me if I had any photos of her mother."

"I will have a drink, and then I will talk to her."

When Henry finished, he knocked on Lizzie's door.

"Can I come in, Lizzie?"

She got up and unlocked the door and went back into bed. An hour later, Henry came out with the promise of taking her riding on Sunday. Ruth looked at Henry.

"She is all right, and I am taking her riding on Sunday."

All day at school, Lizzie looked morose. Not even her friends could cheer her up. She sat by herself and did not converse with anyone. The teacher noticed that she was not listening to the class lessons and appeared preoccupied with her thoughts. Ruth received a note from her teacher and made an appointment to see her the following day.

Ruth arrived at the appointed time and discussed Lizzie's behaviour in the last week. She explained the situation to the teacher.

"I can now understand why Lizzie has been distracted."

"I adopted her at 18 months, and as far as we are concerned, she is our child. However, she was not a simple child to bring up."

"Lizzie is a bright girl," remarked her teacher. "But she does not take her work too seriously. She can be disruptive in class, and she seems to be seeking attention."

Ruth discussed the meeting with Henry.

"Well, we just must do our best with her. Don't worry about it; she will come around."

The first term holiday had started. Both Lizzie and Ruth flew to Hobart. Lizzie was looking forward to seeing her grandmother, and Ruth was anxiously waiting to see Charles and wondering about him; would he recognise her? Would Charles be happy to see her? Had he changed much in his looks?

She continually received news from her mother, who visited him three times a week, and sometimes Ruth's sisters accompanied her.

The following day, Ruth arrived at the hospital with some cookies and books. The matron again greeted her at the door.

"Oh! Mrs Weston, how are you? I have not seen you for a while. Come in, please."

They walked through the corridor to his room. As soon as Charles saw her, he almost jumped out of his bed with happiness. She went over to him, cuddling him heartily with tears in her eyes. She took the presents out one by one; he gobbled the chocolates and handed her a book to read.

Charles appeared quiet and passive overall, and after a few minutes, went to sleep. Ruth called the nurse and spoke to her about him. "He has been, of late, tired and sleeping a lot."

"Did you ask the doctor to have a look at him?" enquired Ruth.

"Yes, on one of his calls, I mentioned it to him, but he just nodded his head, checked his heart rate, and left."

Ruth made an appointment to see the doctor on her next visit.

"Yes," said Dr Andrews, "he has been lethargic and sleeps most of the time. The problem is that his heartbeat is getting slower, and there is nothing much we can do about it."

When she got home, she raised the subject with her mother.

"Yes, I have noticed it as well."

Lizzie was sitting outside.

"Mum, why do you visit him and every time you come home, you cry?"

"He is my son and a human being, and I love him and want the best for him."

"But he can't do anything. He just lies there. Yes, I know he is your son, and I am only adopted."

"Lizzie, that is nonsense. As far as we are concerned, you are our daughter, and you know that."

Ruth was missing not visiting Charles every week. She thought about him constantly, and worried that he might not have adequate care. She was always in touch with her mother. Mrs Callaway noticed that Charles was not eating well but did not inform Ruth. Once, Ruth woke up in the middle of the night feeling that something was wrong with Charles. She kept pacing the floor. In the end, she decided to visit Charles.

The following morning, Ruth told Henry about her anxiety and wish to visit Charles.

"Why don't you ring the hospital? It would make you feel better."

Before she was able to make the phone call, Mrs Callaway rang.

"Hello, Ruth, I have some sad news for you. Charles died last night in his sleep. Dr Andrews rang me this morning. Ruth, it is best for you and Henry. You can both be in peace now."

Ruth burst into tears and gave the phone to Henry.

"We will catch the first boat to Hobart."

"What's wrong, mum?" Lizzie asked.

"Charles died last night in his sleep." Lizzie just sat there, not knowing what to do or say. Henry came over, took Ruth in his arms, and took her to their room to console her.

The following day, Henry went to organise their travel to Hobart. A ship was leaving the next day. When they arrived in Hobart, both of Ruth's sisters met them. Ruth and Henry went to have a last look at Charles.

Two days later, Charles had a private burial followed by morning tea.

A small gathering of the staff from St Mercy, who had taken care of Charles, assembled for afternoon tea at the hospital grounds. It was a bright, warm spring morning. It reminded Ruth of the day she sat outside on the veranda, waiting to see Charles. She could hear the birds singing and rejoicing at the passing of the dark winter days and looking forward to a new dawn. Two days later, they returned home to Sydney. They left their dark secret behind in Hobart.

Part Six

22

Local Personalities of Mosman

Mosman experienced bursts of development, with a significant building boom in 1910. As a result, it became a Federation Suburb, which, in the 1920s and 1930s, created a unique style of design accomplished by Sydney's most skilled architects.

Due to Balmoral Beach's popularity, the Council undertook a major development programme, the Balmoral Beautification Scheme. In 1924, they built the Esplanade, which was extended and lit in the 1930s. In 1929, the Council completed works on the Balmoral Bathers Pavilion, followed by the construction of the Rotunda, overlooking the bay and close to the Rocky Point. A bridge connected the Rotunda area to the Rocky Point Island and was accessible at all times of the tide. The Council also built a shark-proof net to prevent the dangers of an attack.

People of diverse occupations, writers, doctors, artists, and parliamentarians, moved into this much desirable part of Sydney. The neighbourhood became more affluent. Some of them approached Henry to design homes for them, which he did.

One of the first neighbours to move in next to the Westons was Leon Gellert, a well-known poet and journalist, who wrote a column in the Sun-Herald about the eccentricities of Burran Ave and the Rheumatic Society.

Leon loved living in Burran Avenue but could not tolerate outsiders' disturbances of the Avenue's tranquility.

"At the first warm weekend," he wrote, "the oaf comes out of its hiding, and the voice of the lout is heard in the land."

He also wrote columns for various other newspapers, one in Smith's Weekly, 'The Man in the Mask,' dealing with crimes. Another in the Sunday Telegraph, 'Something personal about the goings-on in his Mosman Street,' about Burran Avenue.

However, Leon spent time in Gallipoli, and was repatriated when he became ill.

While he was at home recovering, he wrote his first book of verse, called Songs of Campaign, published in 1917. The Bulletin praised it as the best verse collection produced in the English-speaking world:

"Gellert's sensitive and chilling poems capture the imagination, inspiring empathy for those who remained at home. His evocative descriptions of not only the events at Gallipoli but the feeling of despair, and doggedness of those brave soldiers fueled a sense of national pride."

Leon won the Sydney University's Bunday prize for English Verse, which Angus and Robertson published in an enlarged edition, with illustrations by Norman Lindsay. He then left poetry and joined the Smith's Weekly as a journalist. He later became a director of art in Australia and then moved to the Sydney Morning Herald.

One day, Leon Gellert and his wife were strolling along Mosman Beach with their friend Elioth Gruner, a prominent landscape artist.

As they looked up, they saw two houses standing on top of the cliff, to their surprise. One was a large farmhouse style, and another a smaller but spacious bungalow.

"Who is the owner of those two houses?" asked Leon.

"They belong to Henry Weston," said Elioth Gruner, a commercial artist, "he creates high society posters, which he exhibits on the street fronts of all Tooth and Co. Hotels. He is also well-known for his talent for playing cricket and football. He built this mansion himself and called it 'The Beacon.' He had bought a large piece of land, which he subdivided, and built a small house he rented out to a friend. But, for some reason, their friendship soured, and it is vacant now."

The very next day, Leon met Henry Weston. After some negotiation, and a few glasses of wine, he sold the smaller cottage 'White Lodge' to the Gellerts where they lived for the rest of their married lives. Later, part of Burran Avenue became Stanton Road. Mosman Council finally established a tramline from Military Road to Balmoral.

Creating a road to the beach was not a simple task. After many years of indecision, the tramline was finally constructed. Leon found his paradise, and although the neighbourhood was "if not all agreeable," they were an artistic or a literary lot. Leon built a curved concrete bench and a table closer to the beach for his visitors to view Sydney Harbour's waters. The sand and shallow water shone aquamarine on fine days, but the cobalt blue took over further away from Grotto Point to the Heads. It was a magical sight to behold.

Hugh McCrae, poet and writer, also lived in Mosman and often visited Leon at his home, for they both had a common interest in poetry and literature, which Leon's wife did not appreciate. As Leon wrote:

"My wife, who didn't have sympathy for the ways of poets and artists, did not take to him as wholeheartedly as I did. To put it bluntly, she did not take to him at all. But, when she had shuffled off to bed and was safely beyond earshot, Hugh would let his head go in a torrent of outrageous reminiscences…

> *One sip of gin, however sparing*
> *And I am hopelessly past caring*
> *One inhalation of tobacco*
> *And off the rail I wonder–whacko!*
> *One grain of aspirin, taken orally*
> *And I am acting most immorally*
> *Whereas the deadliest dose of hashish*
> *Just makes me mildly Ogden Nashish.*

John Quin, the most knowledgeable librarian of the New South Wales Parliament and a close friend of Leon, lived in a shack in the southern end of Edwards Beach.

His furniture comprised a trestle table, bench, sofa, bed, piano, ice chest, and gas rings. Quin lived alone, but he invited judges, barristers, politicians, journalists, and other people he knew or his friends for a party, conviviality serving spaghetti bolognaise and Claret on Sundays.

Leonore Goth, a frequent visitor, sang and played on the honky-tonk piano, providing musical entertainment.

In 1931, after Mosman Council claimed Quin's land, he moved to Burran Ave on the other side of the Weston's Beacon, called the Heritage, near the cliff previously owned by Dr Mary Rocke.

Quin changed the name to 'The Chantry' and became a close friend of Leon's. According to Paul Delprat, who grew up in Burran Avenue:

"Quin was a charming bachelor who kept a large jar of boiled lollies in his kitchen for the children from the neighbourhood. Soon his fame spread far and wide, and all the neighbourhood children learnt about his glass jar, which encouraged frequently young visitors to his house. He had a library full of books in the basement, with a strong smell of Four Nun cigarettes."

"On the other side, there were Mr and Mrs Birtles, who lived in a cottage next door to the Westons," narrated Sarah.

"Andrew and I rented a small flat in the basement of the house, overlooking Edwards Beach. Dora was a tall, stately woman with curly hair. She had an English appearance and accent and always had her greying hair tied in a bun. When Dora smiled, she displayed a broad set of her front teeth. Dora swam every morning at Edwards Beach.

"Dora was ahead of her times. She attended Sydney University when only a few women received tertiary education. She wrote several books, short stories, poems and did some travel writing.

"I remember," continued Sarah, "when she returned from Italy once, from one of her travel writing trips, she was so enthusiastic about the country that it made me want to get on the plane immediately. With my earnings, I couldn't have flown to Tasmania.

"She became a member of the International Women's League against Fascism before the Second World War and reported for the Newcastle Sun.

"Mr Birtles had an Australian accent and was short and measured in his opinion with a quiet demeanour. He was sub-editor at the Daily Telegraph, a speechwriter for a parliamentarian in Canberra, and a poet. He also travelled there from time to time when required. They were a pleasant couple.

"I heard," continued Sarah, "they got into trouble when they attended Sydney University and got expelled. Dora wrote a poem on sex, which the literary magazine Hermes published, and Bert Birtles wrote a more explicit poem about their rendezvous on the roof of the university quadrangle.

"They always had parties, and we were fortunate enough to be invited. Most people invited the literati and some eccentrics. I finished with a major and honours in English literature and started teaching. The whole scenario was captivating.

"I remember, one Christmas, Mrs Birtles invited us for morning drinks—people came in Christmas dress-up and she served us homemade mince pies. They were delicious.

"I met one person who came in dressed in his Lederhosen and a Tirolean hat. I thought he was a visitor from Germany. He smiled at me and came and asked me for a dance. He introduced himself as Willy, and he had an Australian accent.

"Willy had just returned from Germany, having spent two years studying language and literature and taught German at Sydney University. He then talked to me in German, and all I could do was laugh. When I told him I studied English literature, he got even more excited and recited German poems with a perfect German accent. It was hilarious".

"At one stage, he began performing as if on stage. He was an eccentric character. I find these characters quite entertaining."

I became very interested in people who display eccentric behaviour, and I started researching this subject.

"Bea Miles was a well-known identity in Sydney in the 50s and 60s," continued Susan. "An iconic eccentric who always travelled in buses and had heated arguments with the drivers. For a small amount of money, she would quote lines from Shakespeare. I occasionally saw her on the bus. Once on my way home from Sydney University, I saw her laden with carrying bags.

"I came across an article in Sydney Morning Herald, a paper clipping on Bea Miles," said Susan. "If you lived in Sydney in the 1950s and early '60s. and regularly travelled through the central business district by tram or taxi, it was impossible not to come into contact with Bea Miles. She often travelled to Balmoral Beach on a bus and spoke to passers-by or recited poems. She was the terror of taxi drivers and tram conductors. Before they knew she was there, she'd be seated in their vehicle, demanding attention, and invariably refusing to pay.

"Miles was the city's iconic eccentric. There she was, advertising her eagerness to quote any passage from Shakespeare (and she appeared to know all the plays and certainly was an expert at all the famous speeches) for no more than sixpence or a couple of shillings. She dressed in a down-at-heel uniform of tennis shoes, a coat that had seen better days and a green tennis hat—and she was belligerent to anyone who didn't treat her with respect. If taxi drivers forced her out of their cabs, she was known to remove doors, jump on the bonnet, or provide unwanted dents by bumping against the sides."

Beatrice Miles was born in Ashfield on September 17, 1902, to William John Miles, an accountant, and his wife, Marie Louise. Miles lived with her family in St Ives and attended Abbotsleigh School for most of her early life. She started an arts degree at Sydney University but abandoned studies after the first year, citing a lack of Australian content in the courses.

After leaving her studies, Miles contracted encephalitis, which possibly exacerbated her arguments with her father, who was appalled by her Bohemian lifestyle and her open advocacy of sexual freedom. He had her committed to the Hospital of the Insane in Gladesville. She remained there for two years.

Miles's reputation was built around her very prominent appearances on Sydney streets. In 1955, for example, she took a taxi from Sydney to Perth and paid £600 for the return journey. Even though she fought with taxi drivers, by the 1940s, she had formed a close relationship with a taxi driver named John Beynon. She was also a regular at the Public Library of New South Wales, until she was banned in the 1950s.

By 1964, ill health dogged her, forced her to retreat to the Little Sisters of the Poor in Randwick, where she died from cancer on December 3, 1973. She told the sisters she had "no allergies that I know of, one complex, no delusions, two inhibitions, no neuroses, three phobias, no superstitions, and no frustrations," when she booked in.

It was a near-perfect bill of health for the city's most famous eccentric.

She had always been a patriot, and, amusingly, her funeral included native wildflowers on her coffin and renditions of 'Advance Australia Fair', and 'Waltzing Matilda', in the spirit of her eccentricity.

"People, generally speaking," continued Susan, "who display eccentric behaviour or quirkiness are often creatively and intellectually gifted, and they are born with a different mindset, which does not necessarily conform to the typical pattern of behaviour. They are unfazed by the opinion of others, and it is hard for people to understand eccentric behaviour as it deviates from the norm."

Part of Mosman Oral History, Paul spoke about his life and growing up in Mosman. Paul grew up in Burran Ave. His family was one of the earliest settlers in the community. His grandfather Howard Ashton, son of Julian Ashton, bought the land from Leason.

After Howard's death, his daughter, Mrs Rosaland Delprat, lived in the Ashton home, and his grandson Paul Delprat built his house with a studio on the grounds. His great grandfather Julian Ashton was an integral part of the history of Australia.

Paul, a delightful and charming man, though a little eccentric, and an artist himself, took over the Julian Ashton Art School after Julian Ashton's death. Tall, handsome, with an open, smiling face, Paul, a well-known Mosman identity, always had time to stop and have a conversation. A raconteur with a penchant for English literature, and the life of the party, Paul had also contributed much to the Mosman community and country. As described by C. Bowman, he was "an iconic Mosman man, a local treasure we should all appreciate."

Unfortunately, Paul had to secede from Mosman Council, undeservedly so, because of political adversity. As a result, he established his kingdom, 'The Principality of Wy.'

In one of my conversations with him, he told me about a shark attack at Balmoral Beach, which he had witnessed. The young boy was dragged deep into the water, although he had managed to swim to the rocks. A little while later, he was dead. He also was one of Paul's friends, which deeply affected him.

Paul talked about his upbringing and his great grandfather Julian Ashton:

"My earliest recollection growing up with Howard was the smell of oil paint, and his palette in his studio, which had a skylight. I remember being fascinated by his palette with the colours, the shiny little tubes, little cylinders of colour, vermillion, the golden yellows, yellow ochre, glossy white, and then the ultra-marine, the depths of the ultra-marine and the cobalt blue. All these beautiful colours and the way he'd draw them with his brush into the body of the palette, smearing it around and then picking it up or sometimes applying it to the canvas with his palette knife. I was, you know, five, six, seven, and these are my earliest memories of, I suppose, things of interest to me. I was surrounded by beautiful paintings, including a marvelous artwork by Norman Lindsay and various other artists."

Paul recalled his school days in Sydney Grammar School, which he attended:

"I did art at school. I was at Sydney Grammar School, and I was drawing all the time. I liked drawing nudes, which has been something that I've done all my life.

I don't know why that is, it's just something that I do. In any case, a French master objected to me doing these nudes and took me up to the headmaster, thinking that perhaps I was going to get a beating.

"The headmaster was an enlightened man—an Oxford scholar, called Mr Healey. I think we called him 'The Rod' for some reason. He told the teacher to get back to his charges and that he would look after me. He examined my drawings. It was a turning point in my life because I thought he was going to whack me. I'd never been hit, but anyway, I was going to be reprimanded for doing these drawings of nudes, you see. And he looked at them and said, 'You know, they're very good, but you don't know anything about anatomy. I've got a book on anatomy here.' He took it down and opened it up. 'See this knee, there's a structure.' I didn't realise what a multi-faceted man he was.

"Then he said, 'Now, I'm going to give you permission to draw in all your classes, but that's something that's got to be between just you and me.' He's dead now, so I can tell this story. 'It's only between you and me, and I will instruct the staff at the next common-room meeting that they are to let you draw, but you are not to tell anybody that.' And so, I had a charmed life through Grammar—I used to draw all the time. I don't know whether the current headmaster would approve of that sort of behaviour there.

"My grandfather, Julian Ashton, developed a great love for this country and the light, and he painted the first en plein air painting, which is exhibited in the Art Gallery of NSW. The first painting that had been painted entirely out of doors, quite a significant picture, it's rather dark, it's interesting. You'd expect it to be full of light, a beautifully luminous painting.

"Ashton went to Melbourne and discovered a group of young painters working at the Heidelberg School. At this stage, Julian was a trustee of the Art Gallery of NSW, and he found paintings from Streeton, McCubbin, Tom Roberts, and Condor. I don't know whether Condor was there when they were painting pictures of the Australian light, so he went back to Sydney, and he said to Montefiori, who was the chairman of the—or the President of the Trustees of the Art Gallery of NSW, 'I will vote for this painting, by this British artist of 'Staggart Bay' or 'Dog with a wet nose', that you want collected; if you will vote for this young artist in Melbourne that I've just discovered, called Arthur Streeton. I particularly want to acquire a painting of his called 'Still glides the Stream and shall forever glide.' It was so poetic, the titles they gave. And if you vote for that, I'll vote for your 'Dog at Staggart Bay.'

"And, of course, Streeton and Roberts subsequently came to Sydney, thinking the streets must be paved with gold, and they set up their camp at Sirius Cove.

"There's a flagpole at Balmoral Beach to mark the position of the campsite, which the excellent Barry O'Keefe, who was Mayor of Mosman for many years, had set up. He was a marvelous person, a patron of the arts, and the President, of course, of the National Trust."

Paul's creative skill had involved him in the movies, The Age of Consent and The Sirens:

"It was a lot of fun—filmmaking is a great art, of course, some of the greatest works of art in our times are films. I remember the Amphitheatre well. As a child,

I used to walk down through the bush with friends. We played balls, and I have a picture of that in my mind.

"Theosophists lived in Clifton Gardens, in an enormous home called the Manor. The Amphitheatre, to me, looked like a picture of a building of the Roman Coliseum. I heard that a very special Indian was coming here, by the name of Krishnamurti. The people in Mosman paid £100 a seat to sit on this concrete platform structure. Krishnamurti was supposed to walk through the Heads to the Amphitheatre. I got very excited and wanted to see how he could walk on water. The only person I heard who walked on water was Jesus Christ in my Sunday School classes.

"The special day arrived, and we all waited in the bush from where we could get an excellent view of the Heads, but he didn't come.

We were all very disappointed. Later, we heard Krishnamurti met a lovely girl on the ship, and they went off to get married, and he never arrived at the Amphitheatre. Well, at least he came to his senses and realised the stupidity of the whole thing."

The Amphitheatre was sold in 1931 and was subsequently used as a theatre for vaudeville and other live performances.

"I remember going there to watch a Shakespearian play, and one gentleman named Walter Kingsley, who had an imposing voice, used to sing there. "

"There was also a mini-golf course on the roof."

"Then, in 1936, the Catholic Church purchased the building, after which it fell into disrepair. Eventually, in 1951, a large red brick building with home units replaced the beach's monumental building. The only change that took place was a facelift to the back of the house facing the street."

Another interesting character who moved to Burran Ave sometime later was Dr Charles Henry Goldfinch, amiably known as Dr Charles. He had lived in Mosman before he went to the Fiji Islands with his dear wife, to work in the tuberculosis hospital in Tamavua for three years.

They enjoyed the lifestyle and the camaraderie, which the expatriate living in Fiji enjoyed. Almost towards the end of his tenure, his wife died of cancer. The head of the hospital asked Dr Charles if he could extend his time in Suva for another three years. He was happy to accept, as there was no reason for him now to return to Australia. Dr Charles had no wife and no children, but now had a maid to take care of household duties and cook his meals. He lived in the most exclusive part of Suva and partook in many social activities.

After his tenure in Fiji, Dr Charles retired and moved back to his home in Mosman. Unfortunately, living alone was not ideal for him as he was not domestically inclined; that had always been his wife's domain. Both his house and garden were in decline. He was an intellectual and spent most of his time reading and researching and often forgot to eat.

He would sit outside on his veranda with his newspaper and breakfast during the weekends. Every time he saw a passer-by, he would raise his cap and greet them:

"Hello, how do you do? Going for a walk? Good for your health."

When he had finished reading his newspaper, he would decide to mow his lawn and do some gardening. He would pull out a few weeds or perform some other gardening activities. However, if there was another passer-by, he would immediately stop to have a chat. Dr Charles knew most of his neighbours, or, more precisely, they knew of him and his quirks.

He would continue to converse with whoever walked past. This would sometimes last all morning, and in the end, he would pack up his tools and leave, refreshed from his monumental garden work.

He often played chess with his next-door neighbour. At the end of the game, they would sit down and have a hearty discussion. There would usually be a heated argument from disagreements between Dr Charles and his friend. However, at the end of the debate, both parties would shake hands, depart with no malice, and look forward to another chess game.

Part Seven

23

Depression and Change

After the First World War and in the ensuing years, life changed throughout the world. The falling wheat and wool prices, and Wall Street's collapse in 1928, caused a worldwide recession. Thousands of people were out of work. Insufficient food, starvation, and increased suicide led to the formation of organisations to help the needy, run mainly by women.

Ruth joined one of these organisations, working tirelessly to provide food, shelter, and clothing. She was putting heart and soul into it. Knitting socks at home was one of her many activities, while raising money for the war effort.

With time, people became more optimistic. There was another influx of immigrants, and the establishment of industries led to an increase in work. A new range of lifestyle changes occurred, such as establishing dance halls for singles. People dressed up, danced to romantic music, and society started relaxing again slowly. Radio and singing became popular together with cinemas. The entire family sitting around and listening to radio plays provided even more family entertainment.

Another factor that changed the ways people used their lifestyle was the invention of cars. The more affluent people who took bushwalks in the countryside now drove their vehicles to the beaches and spent their time picnicking and swimming, especially with the establishment of lifesaving clubs and surf carnivals.

Modernism was an international movement of the 20th century, reacting to changes from industrialisation to modern life. Modernism reached Australia later than Europe and America. It began from about 1914 until 1948; however, Australian Modernism gained significance following the Second World War. Many Australians lost their lives in WWI, but Australia's infrastructure and towns and homes remained intact.

Once again, an influx of immigrants came to Australia from all parts of the world. These immigrants brought with them new ideas, which included modern art. In the early 1900s, female artists from Australia studied in Paris, and the modernist painting style drew them. The artists used materials and techniques in their art forms, demonstrating the changes in modern societies.

Another major event of this era was the emergence of female artists playing a significant role in the art world. During the war, with the lack of male artists, women could be creative and became accepted.

Women's magazines promoted a lifestyle for women, such as political involvement and birth control pills, contributing to their freedom. They became more confident, and the introduction of electrical gadgets allowed them to have more leisure time to pursue other interests.

All this led to the launch of the feminist movement. In Paris and London, Nora Simpson attended the West Minster School of Art, brought back reproductions of modernist art, and introduced them to Australia.

In Paris, she took part at the same art school as Grace Cossington Smith, who created The Sock Knitter in 1914. The idea behind this painting portrayed the quiet work by the women at home to support the war efforts.

Modern art, especially after WWII, developed different styles, including surrealism, social realism, and Expressionism. The avant-garde techniques pushed the boundaries of "status quo" art and used bold, unconventional styles.

Women modernists in Australia used avant-garde techniques and skills. However, as Australia was still a patriarchal society, they were restricted to traditional subjects like still life and interiors, which they found in their homes and gardens. The window which Grace Cossington Smith painted was an excellent example of modernist painting.

Nora Simpson studied art in Australia, then went to Paris, where she met Gauguin, Van Gogh, and Seurat. On her return, she brought back many books and reproductions to show Rubbo's art to school students whose works greatly affected her.

The evolution of new technologies in the 20th century introduced novel ways of creating art, such as etchings in coloured and black-and-white ink in printmaking, lino, and relief painting. Other artists painting in the modernist style were Margaret Preston, Grace Crowley, Roy De Maistre, and Roland Wakelin.

I was ready to move on to the next stage of my life. Other similar companies were opening, and hard times were approaching.

I decided to close my business and use the same space to establish an art school, where I wanted to teach printmaking, etching, and poster designs. I redesigned my workshop into an art school and had in mind to take eight students at a time. I allocated a separate room for my printmaking and etchings.

A large sign hung in front of the building, advertising the art school, and I placed an advertisement in the newspaper. Well-known artists, keen to learn printmaking and etchings, were the first to enrol. With WWII approaching, it was cheaper to sell prints and etchings than large painting.

I received enquiries from young women working in the cities who wanted to take art lessons. These women were keenly interested in modern art. After so many shows of interest, I decided to teach drawing by post. It was an exciting way of teaching. This method of teaching taught the students to draw and not copy. It became very successful, as many students earned money before they completed their course.

About the same time, I built a small timber cottage below my home, using the full view of the beach. I invited my artist friends, such as Norman Lindsay and Howard

Ashton, to spend the weekend painting in the studio. Howard Ashton lived just across from us. Attached to the studio was a small kitchen with a fridge full of beer, a bathroom, and a bedroom.

Often, the artists who stayed for the weekend brought their tents and slept outside. They stopped painting about five, relaxed with a can of beer or more. Settled on the veranda, much laughter ensued.

The artists told jokes, tales from the past. Dr Charles, who also loved painting, joined them occasionally. The noise would increase with his arrival. He was there for camaraderie and entertainment.

One evening, the conversation was on the saga of the Amphitheatre. The construction took place between 1923 and 1924, and there was some talk of selling it.

"I remember the time when the Theosophic Society built the Star Amphitheatre at Balmoral Beach," I said. "The Theosophist Dr Mary Rorke bought the site which had North Head's view at the northern end of Edwards Beach on the hill, taking full advantage of the vista of the beach."

"A monumental building," added Charles, "with semi-circular tiers, seated about 2,000 people, and standing room for another thousand. The building was in a Doric style, white painted proscenium, with pillars facing the beach for the spectators' benefit. It had a stage, a chapel, a tearoom, and a library."

"I went to the opening of it," I said.

"Why on earth would you go to something so ridiculous as that?" asked Dr Charles.

"I was invited by a friend who was a member of the Theosophic Society. And besides, I was curious to experience something new. The Theosophists had invited, supposedly, an exceptional human being who was to become the world leader. They believe that there will appear on earth a human form of God, as a world teacher such as Jesus. Krishnamurti was the human form of the divine."

There was a chorus of laughter from the rest of my friends.

"I can tell you something about this society," said Dr Charles. "When I heard about this divine creature coming to Australia to deliver the message from God, I decided to do some research on him.

"The Theosophical Society was formed in New York in 1875 by a Russian woman called Helena Petrovna Blavatsky, a journalist. But another part of her curriculum vitae was that she was a Russian medium, magician, and circus-rider. The other member in the formation of this society was Henry Steel Olcott, a colonel. It was to be a non-sectarian organisation. The idea behind this organisation was to serve humanity and truth and promote brotherhood. The ideals were based on Hindu and Buddhist philosophies.

"Both these seekers of truth moved to India and lived there for four years. Before Helena died, she created a manifesto of 1,500 pages of sacred doctrine for Theosophy."

"How did it become so strong in Australia?" asked Norman.

"Under the two founders, the Society had flourished in India, America, UK, and Australia," continued Charles. "The headquarters in India was taken over by Anne Besant, a social reformer and Theosophist in Britain. The Sydney Theosophist community was taken over by Charles Webster Leadbeater, an Anglican curate who later became a bishop in the Liberal Catholic Church. He then discovered Theosophy and eventually climbed the ladder, became Annie Besant's chosen one, and moved to Australia in 1914.

"Somewhat territorial, he was eager to move to Sydney to influence society instead of being under Annie Besant's wings. Accused of several misdemeanours in the past, an escape to Sydney, as far away as possible was not a bad idea."

"Do you know how the new leader, Krishnamurti, who was the chosen representative of the Thespian teachings, was to descend on earth and spread the gospel?" asked Charles.

"Vaguely," I said. "You continue, Charles, and enlighten us."

"One day, Mr Leadbeater watched a group of Brahmin children, including Krishnamurti, swimming at the beach. He observed him and was impressed by the size and beauty of his aura. Having watched him, both Besant and Leadbetter agreed that he was the one. They took him under their wings and prepared him for the task that lay ahead. They spread the news and prepared for his arrival."

"The amphitheatre was sold in 1931," continued Charles, "and was subsequently used as a theatre for vaudeville and other live performances.

"I remember going there to watch a Shakespearian play, and one gentleman named Walter Kingsley, who had an imposing voice, used to sing there. Then, in 1936, the Catholic Church purchased the building, after which it fell into disrepair. Eventually, in 1951, a large red brick block of home units replaced the monumental building on the beach. The only change that took place was a facelift to the back of the house facing the street."

"Well, that is an enlightening explanation, from our emeritus Professor Dr Charles. Theosophy appears to be an interesting philosophy, gentlemen, but I think it's time for our barbecue."

Amphitheater at Balmoral Beach. 1924-25

24

A German Gentleman

One day, a foreign gentleman was passing by, when he noticed the sign 'Art School.' He went inside.

"Good morning, I was going past your studio and noticed the sign outside." He spoke English with a strong accent.

"I am also an artist and was curious to see inside your studio. I have just come to Australia and have been in Sydney for a week."

"I am Henry Weston. How can I help you?"

"I am Hans Hermann. I am from Hamburg."

"Hamburg! My parents came from Hamburg in 1870."

"My great-grandfather Hermann Bosse came to Melbourne in the 1850s as a migrant to work in the Ballarat goldfields. He did not find too much gold and eventually decided not to stay. He returned to Germany, married, and had 13 children. One of them was my grandmother. My mother named me after my great-great-grandfather. When I heard those adventurous stories from my grandmother, I always thought that one day I would go to Australia. With the situation in Germany now, it gave me the impetus to migrate."

"My parents," said Henry "left because of the problems they had been experiencing. Australia gave them a chance, and they took it and never had any regrets."

"It must have been very challenging for the migrants to take such a voyage," remarked Hans. "Travelling long distances, fraught with dangers, not knowing what the future holds."

"You have a nice gallery, and I see you do etchings and other things," Hans continued. "I am in Sydney for a couple of weeks to visit a friend but will return to South Australia, where the German community live. I work there, in the winery, and later hope to open my own art studio."

Just then, a couple of customers walked into the studio. Henry liked the young man. He was tall, blond, with very Germanic features, and he reminded him of his father.

"Look, if you are in Sydney over the weekend, I would like to invite you to my home. I have a little artist studio outside the house, and on weekends I invite my friends to paint. Would you like to join us?"

"That sounds wonderful, and very kind of you to invite me. I would very much like to come, but I do not have an easel and painting requirements."

"You don't have to worry about that. I have everything. Would Saturday be suitable?"

"Of course," said Hans.

"Here is my address and phone number. I will see you on Saturday."

Hans arrived on Saturday morning with a bunch of native flowers for Ruth and a few beer bottles for Henry. "Come in, I will introduce you to my wife."

He handed the flowers to Ruth, who was surprised and delighted to receive a beautiful bunch of spring flowers.

"I'll take you to my studio and explain the day's ritual and set up an easel for you."

Norman Lindsay and Howard Ashton arrived; both greeted Henry, who welcomed them heartily and introduced them to Hans. They chatted for a little while and helped themselves to tea, coffee, and biscuits.

"I hope you don't mind, but I am eager to have a close look at the view," said Hans.

"What a beautiful picture of the landscape!" thought Hans, as he went outside to view the scenery.

He came inside, prepared his canvas, and while it was drying, he went outside again to create a mental picture of what he wanted to paint. Then, he returned and started working on his canvas. They stopped to have lunch and a break and continued with their artwork.

They stopped at five, gathering around Hans to see what he had produced. "Your style of painting is leaning towards Expressionism," said Howard. "It is very subjective. I like what you have done, the beauty of the seascape in the background, the suffering people in the front."

"An exciting painting," remarked Howard.

They walked to the veranda and got their beers out. It was a hot day. Luckily Henry had installed a ceiling fan in the studio. However, outside on the patio, a cool breeze was blowing. Just then, Dr Charles arrived in his usual cheerful spirit, greeting everyone.

"Charles, come and meet Hans, whom I met at work."

"Welcome, Hans. What made you come to Australia?"

"My great-grandfather came to work in the Ballarat goldfields and had many tales to tell in his letters he wrote home."

"I have a humorous story to tell," said Dr Charles.

"There was a man in the goldfields, called 'Dandy of the diggings.' You probably don't know what a dandy is, Hans. He is a person dressed extravagantly in a stylish manner. However, this one was dressed in a long red frock top, with a broad shiny belt, and from it hung a large pistol on a brass hook around his waist. He wore a broad hat with a black ribbon attached to it. He had black whiskers and a moustache, which he carefully brushed and curled, in keeping with the fashion.

"When he was happy with his attire and his groomed look, he stepped forward. He saw a digger passing by and asked him if he would carry his bag of sugar from his cart to his tent, which was only a distance of 27 metres. For that, he would pay him a shilling. The digger looked at him disdainfully and, putting his foot on a stone, said, 'Listen mate, if you tie my bootlace, I will give you a crown.' Not expecting such an answer, the dandy quickly picked up his bag of sugar and bolted while the bystanders had a good laugh."

They all laughed. "You have a joke for every occasion," said Henry.

"Yes, I am a collector of jokes."

"What is happening in the art world in Germany?" enquired Henry.

"Modernism is gaining popularity in Germany. Naturally, Impressionism still appeals to many. The idea behind Expressionism is not to create a realistic and beautiful portrayal of life, but to express strong emotions to the world around you. The artists looked at art subjectively.

"In 1905, a few German students set up a group with Ernst Ludwig Kirchner's help, who named it 'Die Brücke.' In 1911, Kandinsky and Franz Mark formed a Munich group called 'Der Blaue Reiter.' They were more interested in using colour and form to express spiritual values.

"Unfortunately, when Hitler came to power, he did not like the modern style of painting and identified it with the Jewish people. He called it a degenerate art by an inferior race and banned this form altogether, reverting to Greek and Roman art."

"What about Aboriginal art?" said Hans.

"I read about an Aboriginal artist called Albert Namatjira from a place called Hermannsburg in central Australia. I have seen his paintings of the Macdonald Ranges, which are very well executed. He attended a Lutheran school in Hermannsburg after he and his family became Lutherans. He must have been very talented— he picked up painting by observation."

"Namatjira sketched scenes of the cattle-yards, hunters, stockmen, and anything he found interesting around him from an early age," added Hans.

"Rex Battarbee," said Dr Charles, "was the artist who came to paint in Hermannsburg and discovered his talent. He took him to the MacDonald Ranges, where he painted many scenes. Namatjira was able to make some money but remained true to his culture."

"He was one of the rare ones," said Dr Charles. "They generally lived in isolation within their tribe; they didn't have a culture of painting or culture at all. They were uncivilised until the white men came to this country. They ran around naked. Their children were covered in flies, their noses running. They spread diseases as they lived under unhygienic conditions. They did not wash themselves. Their lifespan was limited."

"The aboriginal culture is one of the world's oldest, at least 40,000 years old," said Henry. "A nomadic race with simple possessions, they moved seasonally for not only food but to join with another tribe to perform rituals and ceremonies. They were hunters and gatherers. Men hunted for their food, while women would collect plants, berries, and fruit. They lived in small communities.

"The white man did not respect nor try to understand their culture. Many died of diseases and smallpox, which was introduced by the white settlers. Many Aborigines were killed during the fighting and skirmishes with the Europeans.

"The design in all aboriginal art forms is tied up with religious beliefs and myths. They do not have a written history, but their culture and history, knowledge of the land, events, and beliefs, are passed through a rich oral tradition of storytelling in their song-poetry and legends.

Their land is sacred to them. They use earth colours, such as red-ochre, yellow-ochre, and charcoal from the campfires to paint their bodies, known as body art, for ceremonial purposes.

"They have painted their carvings, rock faces, barks of the trees and their totems, with designs that told the creation stories they learned from their ancestors and passed on from one generation to another.

"Cave paintings were the earliest art form, discovered in Egypt and in France. The oldest cave painting was found on the wall in a cave in Lascaux, in France. The Aborigines used their cave paintings to communicate, to tell their stories known as 'dreaming.'"

"They do beautiful bark paintings," added Hans. "I have seen some very interesting ones in the museum in South Australia. They are mostly from Arnhem Land and the Gulf of Carpentaria. Their art of crosshatching and dotting is remarkable. They make their fixative using orchid juice. The pigments, mainly red and yellow, kaolin and charcoal are crushed and mixed with water, and they use frayed or chewed twigs or a feather to apply the paint."

"You seem to have done some research into Australian history," said Henry.

"Yes, I did some reading before I left for Australia. When I arrived in South Australia, I went to the library to get myself acquainted with the land and its customs."

"It is very simplistic to call this art," said Charles. "I can understand if their so-called art form is part of their religion, legends, and creation stories, but I cannot see them as an expression of an art form. They are too childlike, and anyone can do them. Art, to me, is much more complicated in its execution and the thinking behind it. It expresses one's own ideas and thoughts."

"In Tasmania", said Henry, "there was an Aboriginal reserve near our home. The government tried to protect the Aboriginal people, and their dwindling population, by establishing a protectionist policy, which lasted from 1880 to 1930. They were isolated in reserves and church missions, given food, clothes, and blankets. My wife was very much involved with them. They sometimes received a basic education. The squatters and the settlers also used them as cheap labourers on their farms and land. As a young child, I used to play with Aboriginal children. Close to our farm, there was a creek, and my father took me there to teach me how to swim. The boys used to gather around him, and my father taught them some English words."

"It's time for the barbecue," said Henry. Tom and Howard did the barbecue. Ruth had already prepared the potatoes with foil, and Henry and Hans set the table.

Part Eight

25

Lizzie's Life

Lizzie continued with schooling and managed to finish it. She was in limbo, as far as her future was concerned. She spent most of her time at Balmoral Beach, swimming, sunbathing, and socialising. The Rotunda at Balmoral Beach was a meeting place for her friends.

It was January, and she did not try to find work.

"Lizzie, school days are over, and so is the holiday. Now you must think about finding some work," said Ruth. "What is it you are interested in doing?"

"I don't know what I want to do. I would like to go overseas and travel. My friend, Joan is very keen to travel, and we could maybe do it together."

"How about you first do a business course in the city, get a job, work for six months, and we will pay for your trip overseas and give you some money for living expenses. In this way, you can get a job in London and save some money to travel in Europe."

"All right, I will think about it." The following day, Lizzie spoke to Joan, "Oh! what a great idea, let's do it." They both enrolled simultaneously, finished the business certificate, worked for six months, saved some money, and started dreaming about their future travels.

When Lizzie finished her course, which she enjoyed and received excellent results for, she applied to work in a solicitor's office.

She worked for two years in the same place, which was much longer than planned, as she enjoyed her work. She saved up enough money and left for England.

Joan was already working in England; she met Lizzie on her arrival. Together, they rented a more spacious apartment and spent a week discovering London. Lizzie applied for a job once again in a solicitor's office. She had no trouble being accepted within the legal profession with her credentials.

Lizzie enjoyed her work; she met many people her age but did not find a beau to take home to Australia. She had already decided that she would never marry and have children. Lizzie had no inclination for that lifestyle but loved cats. She chose to have cats for company and be her own master of her destiny. She travelled a lot, enjoyed life to the fullest, and joined the Australian Club. She loved London and her lifestyle. She aimed to remain indefinitely in London, for she loved her work and lifestyle.

However, it was not to be. Lizzie received news from her father that her mother was seriously ill and she should come home. She packed her luggage, said goodbye to London, and left for home after being away for six years.

When Lizzie arrived back in Sydney, she found out that her mother had cancer.

"Lizzie, I am so happy to see you. How have you been? How was the travelling? How was London? Tell me everything. I missed you so much."

Tears came gushing out of Lizzie's eyes. She hugged her mother, who looked pale and very thin.

"You look so well, Lizzie. London must have suited you."

"Who is your doctor?" asked Lizzie.

"Dr Carlson."

"That handsome doctor—is he married?" Lizzie asked with a twinkle in her eyes.

"Not now," Ruth replied with a smile. "He has been married three times previously, I think."

A few days later, Ruth died. Lizzie was happy that she was home and could spend this valuable time with her mother.

Memories of the past flooded her mind. She realised how kind, caring, and loving Ruth had been to her. However, Lizzie could not get over the fact that she was an orphan.

Lizzie wanted to try something different and needed a change. Her eyes stopped at an advertisement for a receptionist to work for Dr Carlson. The previous receptionist was on maternity leave but was taking an extended break. She applied, and after an interview and with her work experience, she got the job.

Lizzie enjoyed her work, but more than that, she enjoyed the company of Dr Carlson. Often, she stayed behind and helped him with his work. Lizzie was competent and learned to assist Dr Carlson with minor operations he performed. One day, Lizzie told Dr Carlson that her father of late wasn't looking too well.

"It could be due to him missing your mother," remarked Dr Carlson.

"He has lost weight, and I am a bit worried about him."

"If you like, I am happy to come over and have a look at him."

"That's very kind of you. Would you like to come and have dinner with us?"

"If that's an invitation, I will accept."

It was Saturday, and Lizzie was expecting Dr Carlson for dinner. There was a knock at the door. She looked out of the window and saw him with an enormous bunch of flowers. "This is the man I am going to marry, even though he is 15 years older than me."

And she did, with a lavish party given at her Mosman home.

Lizzie wanted to stay at her house, but Dr Carlson insisted that they live in his home. Lizzie continued to work and take care of her dad. One afternoon, she visited her father after work and found him still in bed.

On a closer look, Lizzie realised he was not moving. She telephoned Percy, who came straight away.

"I am sorry, Lizzie. Your father died in his sleep."

After the death of Henry Weston, Lizzie was now the owner of the Beacon, the mistress of the most beautiful house in Mosman. Lizzie and Dr Carlson moved into her home. She was the lady of the Manor. The first thing Mrs Carlson did was sell most of her parents' furniture. With part of the money, she refurnished her home with French antiques, a provincial sofa with matching armchairs, crystal chandeliers, bedside tables, and a large mahogany eight-seater dining table and chairs.

Lizzie loved cats. Unfortunately, she could not have any when Ruth was alive, as she was allergic to them.

She started filling her home with cats, one by one until she had nine of them. Lizzie had a room full of cots where the cats slept. They were her children. She drove to Sydney University Veterinary Hospital for treatment if one cat fell ill.

She employed a gardener to care for the garden, who lived in her father's studio. A designer jewellery shop had just opened in Mosman, and out of curiosity, she visited the shop. The dazzling array of stones, that she had never seen before, delighted her. A beautiful one-carat diamond ring flashed before her eyes. Her mother did not wear jewellery, so she could not inherit any.

Overcome by the beauty of these crown jewels, she sold a piece of her land to raise money. Lizzie placed a caveat on it; the owners were not allowed to build above the stipulated height of her bedroom. After all, she did not need the piece of land, but she did need some jewellery.

Lizzie found a friend in the jewellery shop, and a friendship developed between three of them, including her husband. They were at her beck and call. They were there to grant her every wish. Lizzie promised them her home after her death, as she had no next kin. They often came and stayed with her, did whatever she asked of them, and took care of her. They travelled together all over Australia. Unfortunately, a rift developed between them, which ended their friendship.

The house next door to Lizzie was completed after many complaints from Lizzie regarding the construction of the house on the land she sold. However, the new owners needed to leave for Singapore for work. The owners rented their home to an Indian doctor with a wife and two children.

They had just arrived in Sydney from India. Dr Gupta, a specialist, took a position at the North Shore Hospital.

Lizzie kept a careful watch over them. Dr Gupta, a kindly gentleman with a warm smile, introduced himself, but he only received a silent nod.

"I owned that property, you know. Make sure you look after it."

"Don't worry, Mrs Carlson. We will." Dr Gupta went home and told his wife.

"I think that woman will cause a lot of trouble, so be careful."

The next day, Lizzie could smell something erupting from next door. What is that smell? she wondered. She got up and went to investigate and knocked on the door. Suneel, their son, opened the door.

"Hello, Mrs Carlson."

"Is your mother home?" Lizzie asked in a stern voice.

"I will go and get her," he said politely.

Meena greeted her with a friendly smile. "Would you like to come in?"

"No, certainly not. What is the smell that I am inhaling coming from the house?"

"Oh!" said Meena, "I am making curry, and it must be the spices you are smelling."

"Well, I have never smelled anything so awful. Please keep your doors and windows closed when you do your cooking." With that, she left.

The following day, Meena decided to cook some extra food and take it to Lizzie. She made a parcel, placed it inside a basket, knocked on the door, and left.

Lizzie opened the door and was surprised to find the basket; she took it inside and showed her husband what she had seen.

"Oh! That's wonderful. We can have that for lunch," he said. "It is Indian food and very tasty," he added. By now, Dr Carlson had retired and was not in good health.

"I don't know if I am going to like this food," said Lizzie.

"Lizzie, you will like it, I am sure. You must try it."

"Well, it is very different," she said.

Lizzie returned the basket and dishes the following day but left them outside Meena's door.

"I think she must have liked the food," said Meena when her husband came home.

"Why don't you leave some food for her outside her door, once a week, or whenever you like?"

So, this ritual continued to take place.

One day, Dr Gupta was outside the house with his wife.

"Good morning, Dr Carlson. You are on your usual walk?"

"Good morning. Thank you for the delicious food. We have really enjoyed it. Come and have a drink with us one evening."

"Thank you, sir. That would be nice," said Dr Gupta. Lizzie had little to say except "thank you," and they went on their way.

With time passing, many changes took place in Mosman. Large pieces of land were sold, and many more houses built. Mosman and its environs became more and more developed. Balmoral Beach gained popularity, attracting people from all parts of Sydney.

After the death of Dr Carlson, Lizzie survived for another 15 years. She lived on her own; her only companions were her cats. When she died, she bequeathed her estate to the veterinary hospital in Sydney. Not long after her death, the Beacon was sold.

History continues in the house with new owners. The one painting they left behind, hanging on the wall, will always serve as a reminder of the Westons and their life at the "Beacon."

Bibliography

Aboriginal Mosman, Mosman Council Research Paper, 2000, Local Studies

A History of Germans in Australia, 1839-1945, Monash University, Clayton (Victoria), Wynyard, Centre for Tasmanian Historical Studies

A Brief History of Mosman, Mosman Council, Mosman Library Services Local collection, updated 2021

Barnard Marjorie. A History of Australia, Angus and Robertson Publishers, quote page 396, 90 words, 1962

Adoption, Find and Collect, Tasmania, https://wwwfindandconnect. gov.au

Appeldorff, Gwendolyne. Memories of Collinsvale, Forty Degrees of South Pty Ltd, Hobart Publishers,1986

Bohemians in the Bush, The Artists Camps of Mosman, 1991, produced by Art Gallery of NSW

Braye Donna, Bohemians in the Bush, Mosman Library 1991, https://en.wikipedia.org/w/index.php

Caban Geoffrey, A Fine Line: A History of Australian Commercial Art, Black and White etchings by Henry Weston, Hale and Iron Monger, UNSW,1983

Dictionary of Sydney, Charity, and Philanthropy, 2008

De Vries-Evans Susanna, Conrad Martens, On the Beagle and in Australia, 1993 Pandanus Press

Early Construction and Heritage Properties, 1900-1930, Website search

Gellert Leon. A Torrent of Words, A Writer's Life,1996, Canberra Press

German Australia, Tasmania, Tasmania German Speaking immigration to Australia in the 19ᵗʰ Century - overview, A History of Germans.

German Speakers in Australia, 1835-1945, Monash University, Victoria, Website German Australia, Tasmania, Tasmania German Speaking immigration to Australia in the 19ᵗʰ Century - overview, A History of Germans, Website, German Australian

Great Depression of Australia, Defining Moments, National Museum of Australia, 1930 Website

Madness and insanity: A history of mental illness from evil spirits to modern medicine, abc.net.au

Roberts Tom. National Gallery of Australia, 1856-1931

Souter Gavin, Mosman 1994 A History, Melbourne University Press

Sydney Artists' Camps Wikipedia, 2019Knoblauch, Beat coll. Sydney Views, 1788-1888,

The Bulletin Debate, Wikipedia.orgThe World of Norman Lindsay, Black and White etchings by Norman Lindsay for The Bulletin,1979. Bloomfield, Macmillan press. The Companion to Tasmanian History, 2005. University of Tasmania

The companion to Tasmanian History, Thematic studies-Gender, 200. Centre of Tasmanian Historical Studies

The companion to Tasmanian History, Adult Education, 2006, Centre of Tasmanian Historical Studies

Williams, Donald. In Our Own Image. The Story of Australian Art, 1788-1989, McGraw-Hill Book Company

Acknowledgement

The idea of writing Visions from the Past was inadvertently placed in my mind by my neighbour, Paul Delprat. Paul, a descendent of Julian Ashton from a line of an eminent family, a raconteur, entertained and enlightened me with stories and intriguing tales about the people and the famous artists who worked in campsites at Edwards Bay and Sirius Cove. When I heard these interesting, remarkable stories, My creative spirit overcame me and a novel started shaping in my mind. However, many years passed before I put pen to paper. I realised Mosman has such an exciting and artistic history, and it should be revealed not as a textbook but as a historical novel. I thank Paul for inspiring me to write this book.

'Many hands make light work.' My sincere thanks and gratitude to Christine Gartelmann, for so generously giving up her time, reading my drafts and for her guidance and support whenever I needed them. Susan Kelly for her enthusiastic support, for providing me with interesting historical material, and entertaining me with her anecdotes and humorous tales. Munday has been part of my writing life and has read all my drafts. I thank her once again for her support and friendship. I also thank Pieter Bierkens, Jill Knoblauch, Paul Delprat and Sue Delprat for their valuable comments.

To my family, especially Kiran Colpani, for translating a part of my chapter into Australian Strine – Slang. Justin Colpani for his contribution. Last but not least I want to thank Carlo for his love, dedication and support and getting me through difficult times during my writing of Visions from the Past.

.CPSIA information can be obtained
at www.ICGtesting.com
Printed in the USA
BVHW020427121022
649152BV00020B/942

9 781636 406534